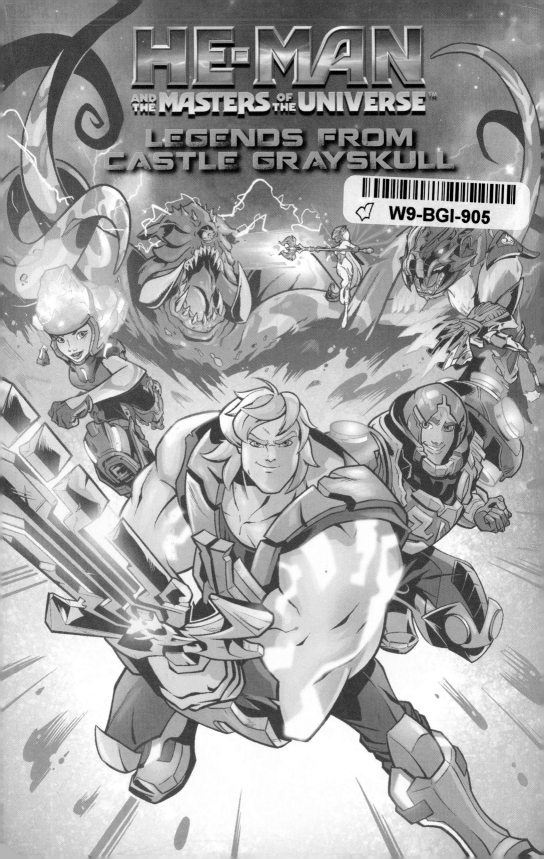

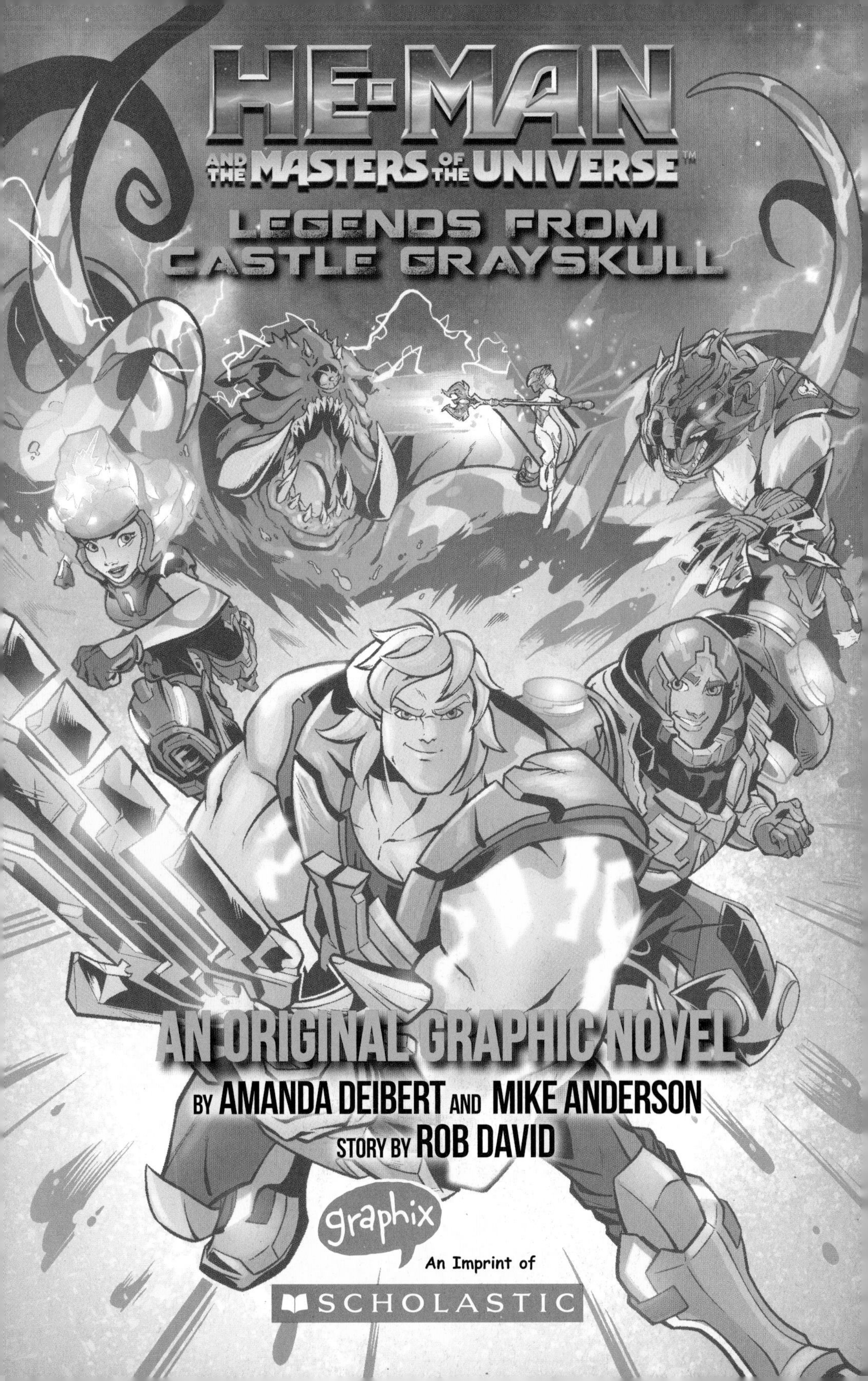

HE-MAN AND THE MASTERS OF THE UNIVERSE™

LEGENDS FROM CASTLE GRAYSKULL

AN ORIGINAL GRAPHIC NOVEL

BY AMANDA DEIBERT AND MIKE ANDERSON
STORY BY ROB DAVID

graphix
An Imprint of
SCHOLASTIC

ISBN 978-1-338-74549-8

10 9 8 7 6 5 4 3 2 1   22 23 24 25 26

Printed in the U.S.A.   40

First printing 2022

Illustrator: Mike Anderson

Colorist: Brad Simpson

Lettering: Dezi Sienty

Book design by Jeff Shake

Edited by Lori Wieczorek

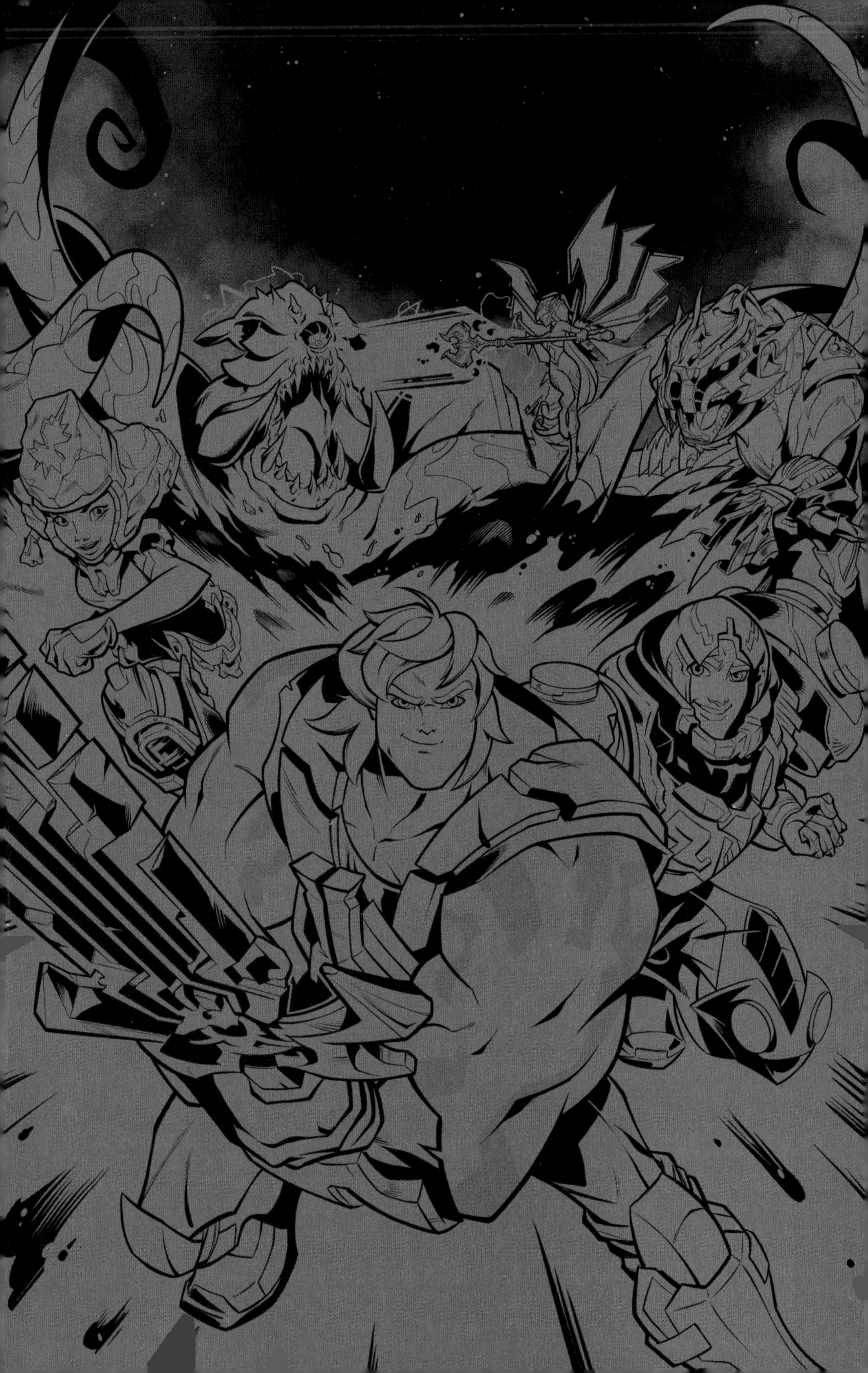

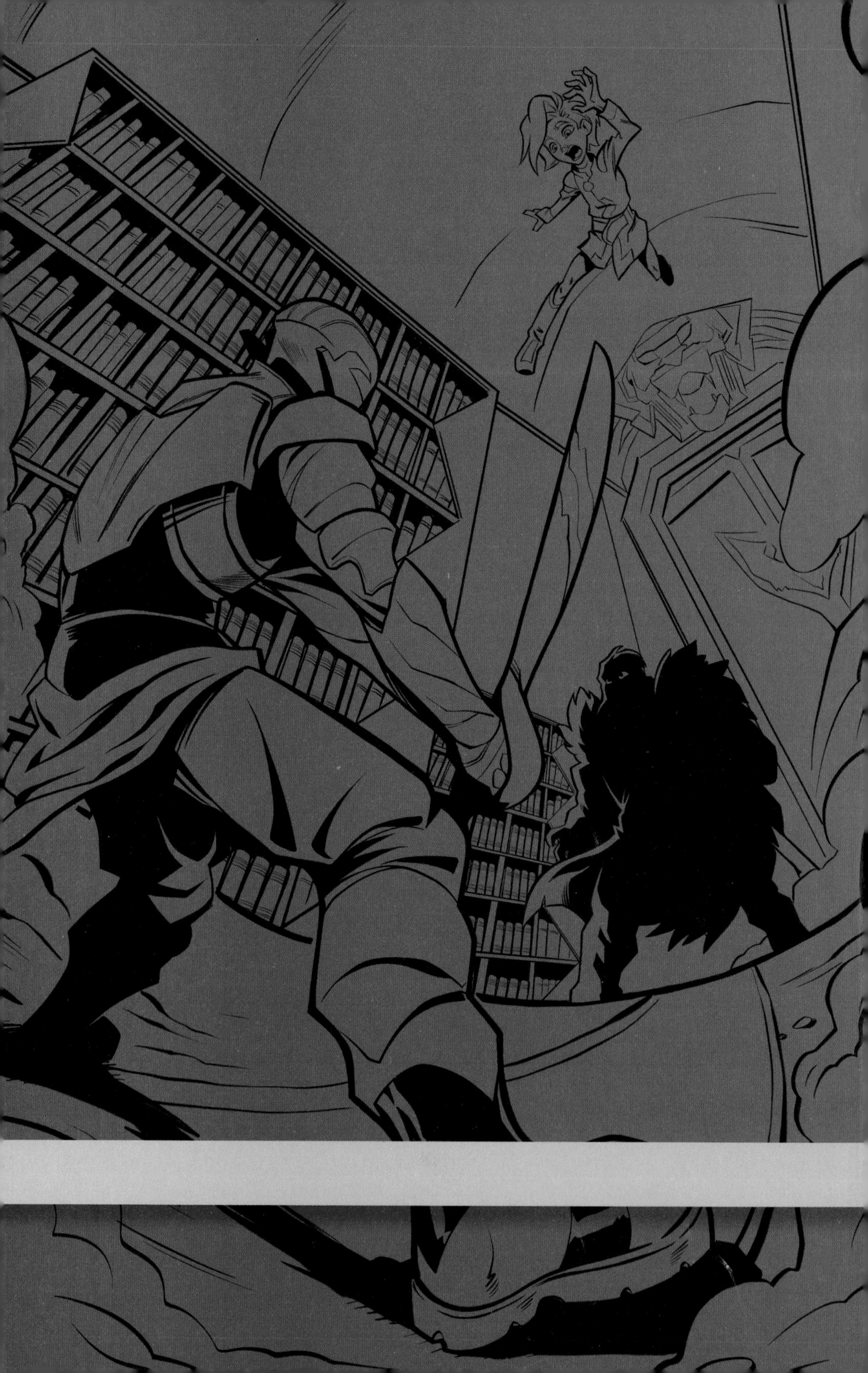

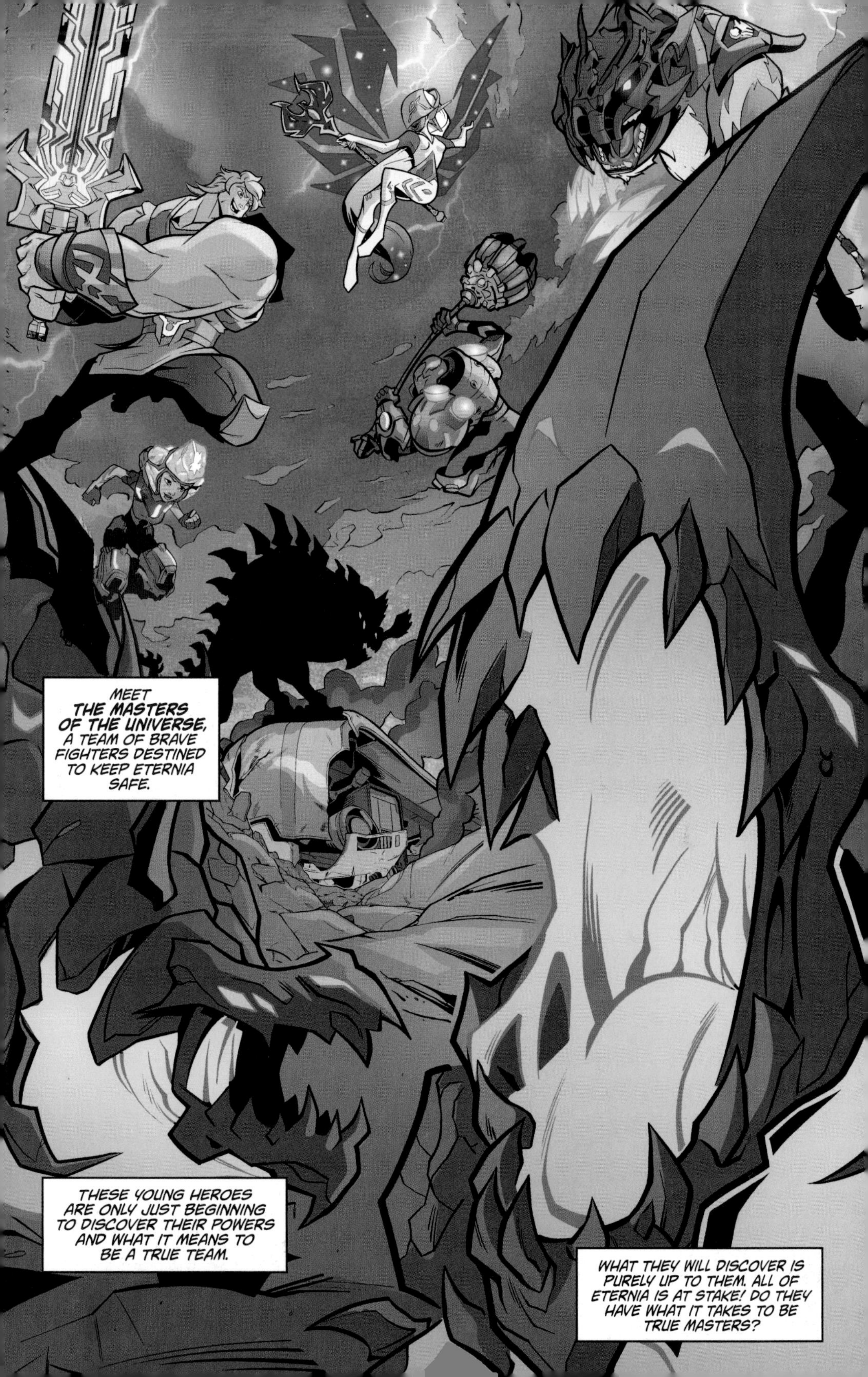
MEET THE MASTERS OF THE UNIVERSE, A TEAM OF BRAVE FIGHTERS DESTINED TO KEEP ETERNIA SAFE.
THESE YOUNG HEROES ARE ONLY JUST BEGINNING TO DISCOVER THEIR POWERS AND WHAT IT MEANS TO BE A TRUE TEAM.
WHAT THEY WILL DISCOVER IS PURELY UP TO THEM. ALL OF ETERNIA IS AT STAKE! DO THEY HAVE WHAT IT TAKES TO BE TRUE MASTERS?

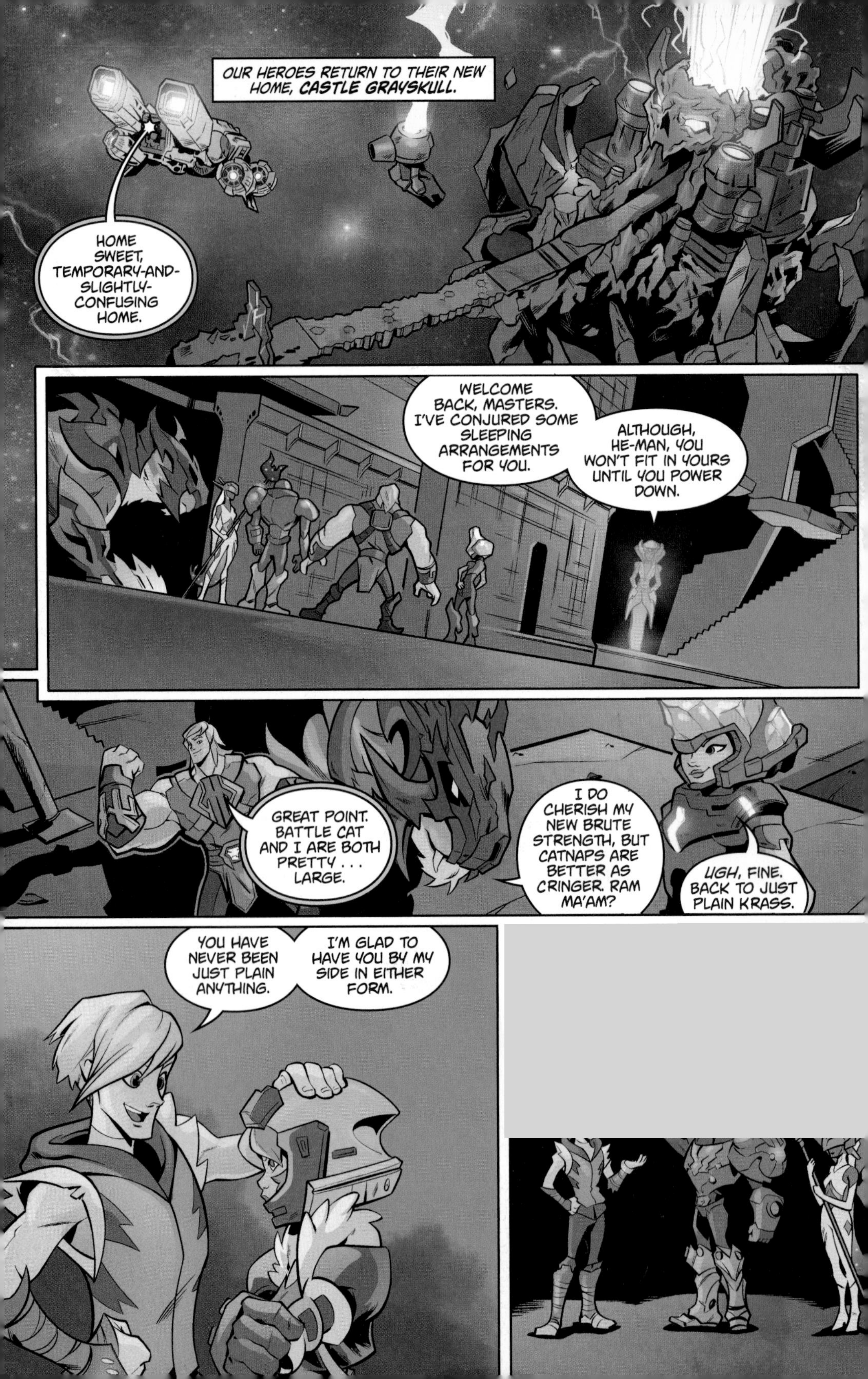
OUR HEROES RETURN TO THEIR NEW HOME, CASTLE GRAYSKULL.
HOME SWEET, TEMPORARY-AND-SLIGHTLY-CONFUSING HOME.
WELCOME BACK, MASTERS. I'VE CONJURED SOME SLEEPING ARRANGEMENTS FOR YOU.
ALTHOUGH, HE-MAN, YOU WON'T FIT IN YOURS UNTIL YOU POWER DOWN.
GREAT POINT. BATTLE CAT AND I ARE BOTH PRETTY . . . LARGE.
I DO CHERISH MY NEW BRUTE STRENGTH, BUT CATNAPS ARE BETTER AS CRINGER. RAM MA'AM?
UGH, FINE. BACK TO JUST PLAIN KRASS.
YOU HAVE NEVER BEEN JUST PLAIN ANYTHING.
I'M GLAD TO HAVE YOU BY MY SIDE IN EITHER FORM.

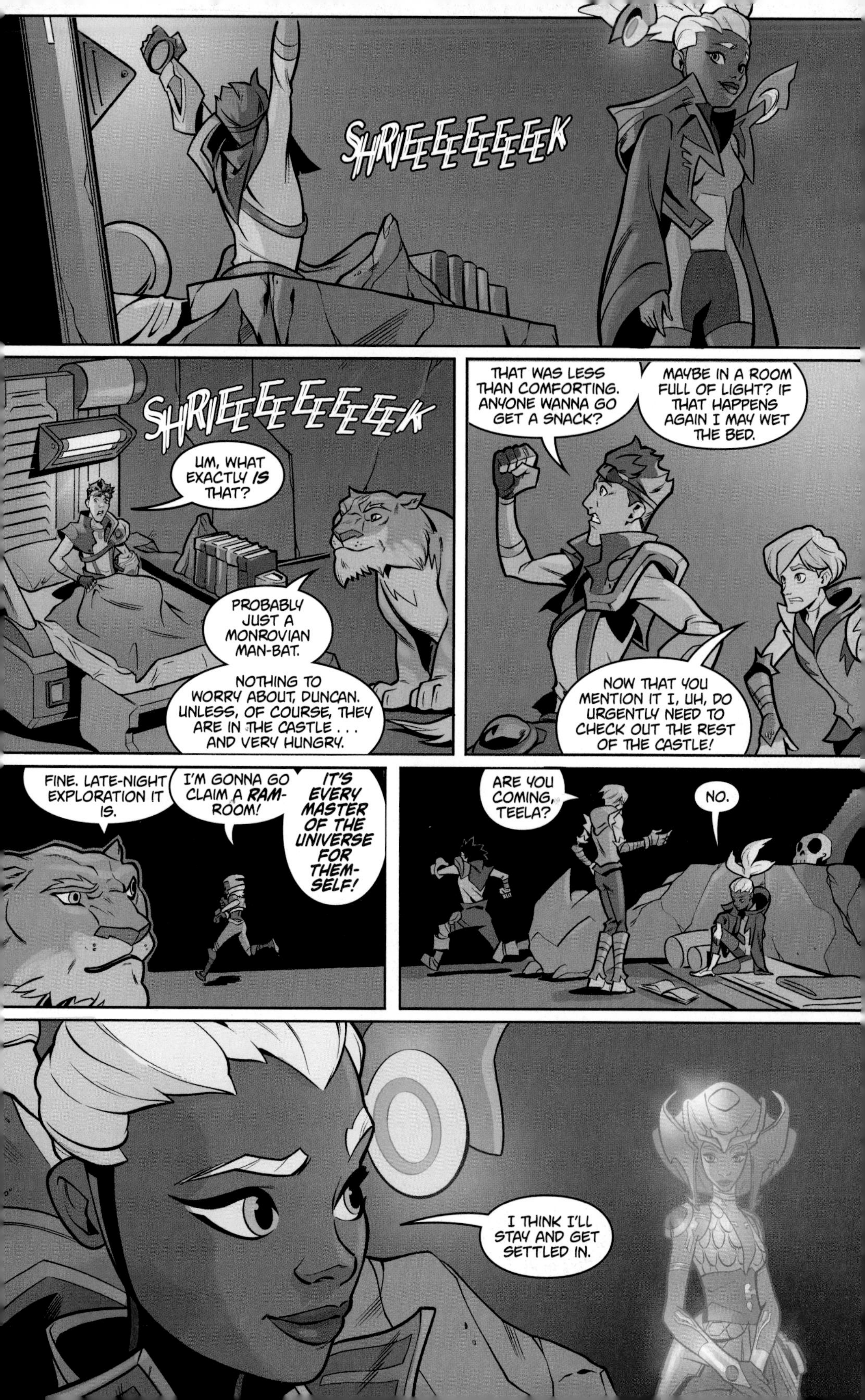
SHRIEEEEEEEEEEK
SHRIEEEEEEEEEEK
UM, WHAT EXACTLY *IS* THAT?
PROBABLY JUST A MONROVIAN MAN-BAT.
NOTHING TO WORRY ABOUT, DUNCAN. UNLESS, OF COURSE, THEY ARE IN THE CASTLE . . . AND VERY HUNGRY.
THAT WAS LESS THAN COMFORTING. ANYONE WANNA GO GET A SNACK?
MAYBE IN A ROOM FULL OF LIGHT? IF THAT HAPPENS AGAIN I MAY WET THE BED.
NOW THAT YOU MENTION IT I, UH, DO URGENTLY NEED TO CHECK OUT THE REST OF THE CASTLE!
FINE. LATE-NIGHT EXPLORATION IT IS.
I'M GONNA GO CLAIM A *RAM*-ROOM!
IT'S EVERY MASTER OF THE UNIVERSE FOR THEMSELF!
ARE YOU COMING, TEELA?
NO.
I THINK I'LL STAY AND GET SETTLED IN.

SUIT YOURSELF. I NEED TO . . . EXPLORE.

STILL HAVEN'T FOUND THE BATHROOM?

NOPE!

PLEASE BE IT!

HELLO? ANY TOILETS?

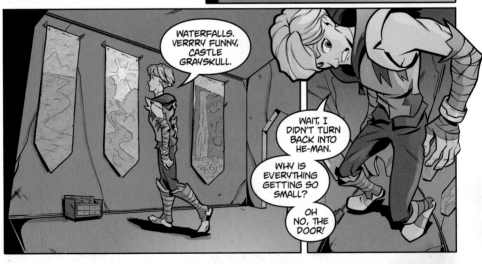

WATERFALLS. VERRRY FUNNY, CASTLE GRAYSKULL.

WAIT, I DIDN'T TURN BACK INTO HE-MAN.

WHY IS EVERYTHING GETTING SO SMALL?

OH NO, THE DOOR!

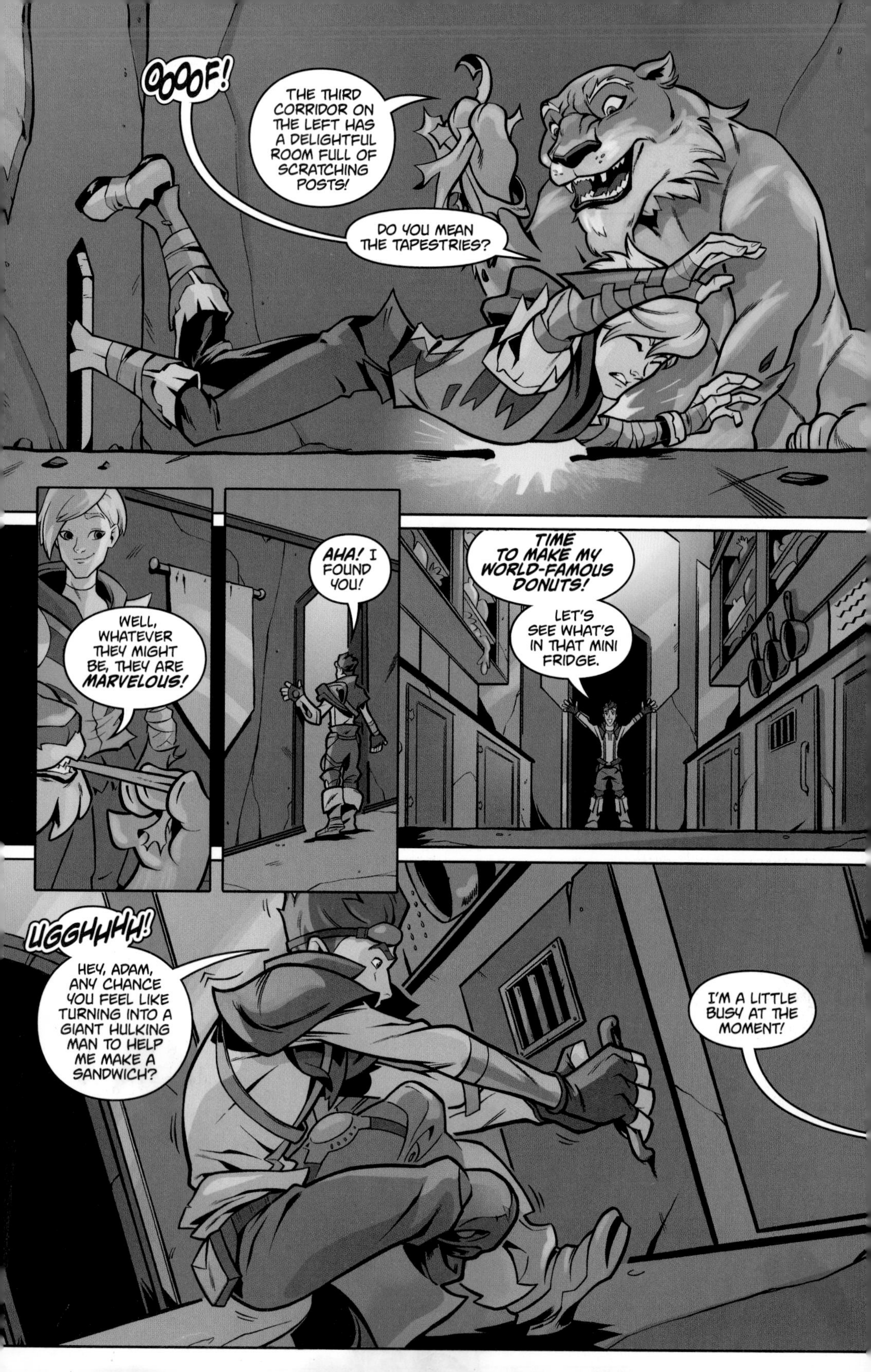
OOOOF!
THE THIRD CORRIDOR ON THE LEFT HAS A DELIGHTFUL ROOM FULL OF SCRATCHING POSTS!
DO YOU MEAN THE TAPESTRIES?
WELL, WHATEVER THEY MIGHT BE, THEY ARE MARVELOUS!
AHA! I FOUND YOU!
TIME TO MAKE MY WORLD-FAMOUS DONUTS!
LET'S SEE WHAT'S IN THAT MINI FRIDGE.
UGGHHHH!
HEY, ADAM, ANY CHANCE YOU FEEL LIKE TURNING INTO A GIANT HULKING MAN TO HELP ME MAKE A SANDWICH?
I'M A LITTLE BUSY AT THE MOMENT!

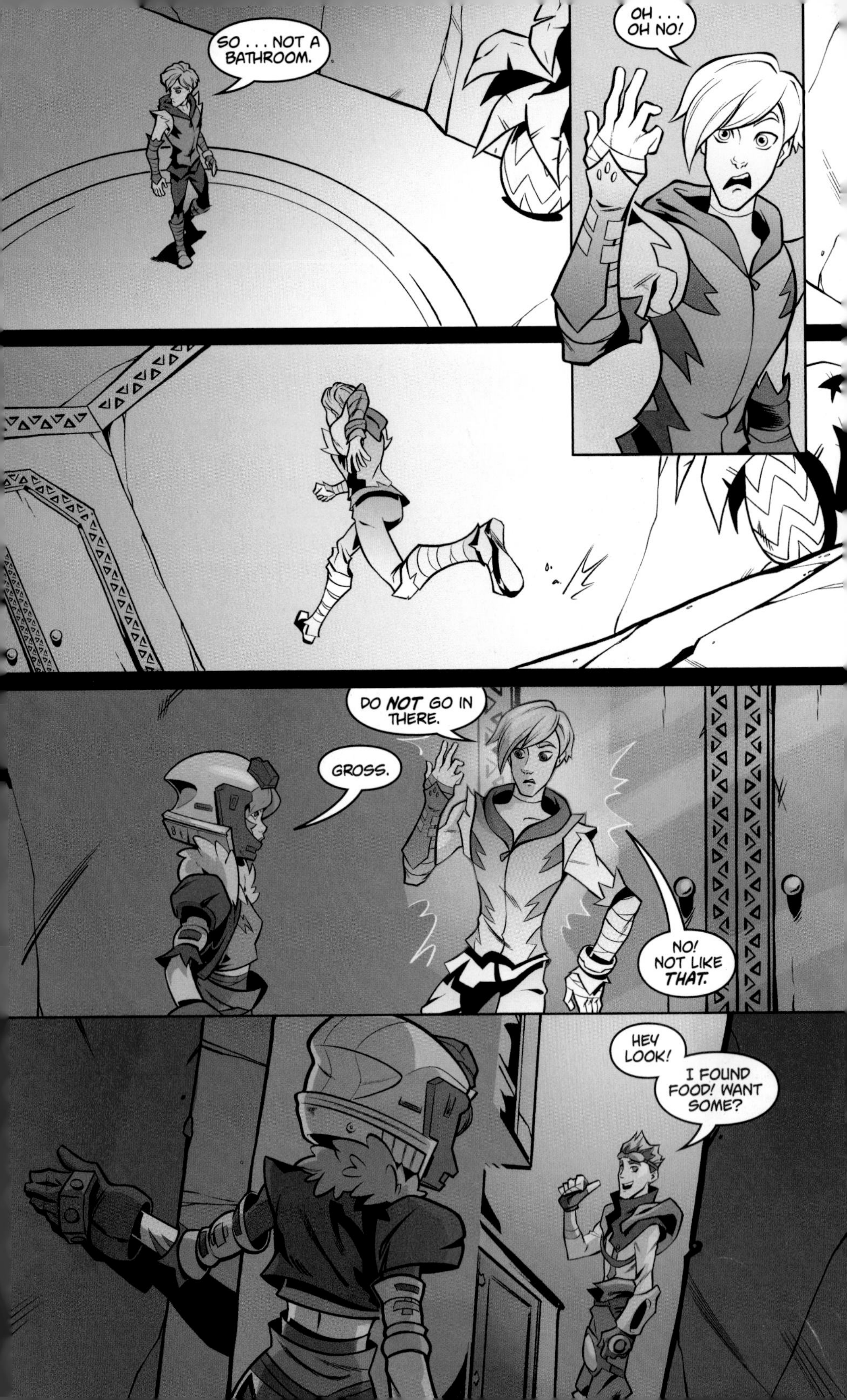
SO . . . NOT A BATHROOM.
OH . . . OH NO!
DO NOT GO IN THERE.
GROSS.
NO! NOT LIKE THAT.
HEY LOOK!
I FOUND FOOD! WANT SOME?

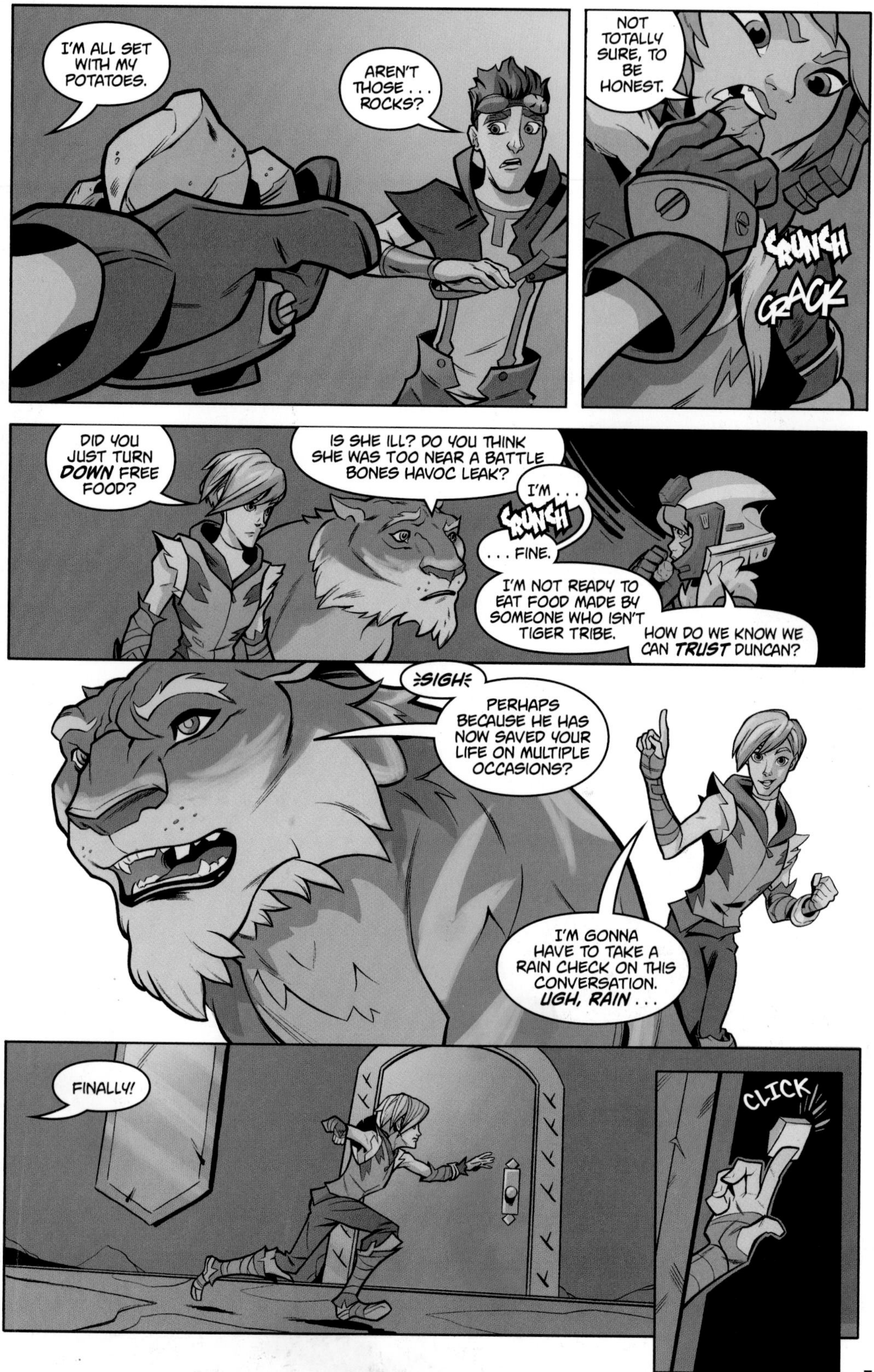
I'M ALL SET WITH MY POTATOES.
AREN'T THOSE . . . ROCKS?
NOT TOTALLY SURE, TO BE HONEST.
SRUNCH
CRACK
DID YOU JUST TURN DOWN FREE FOOD?
IS SHE ILL? DO YOU THINK SHE WAS TOO NEAR A BATTLE BONES HAVOC LEAK?
I'M . . .
SRUNCH
. . . FINE.
I'M NOT READY TO EAT FOOD MADE BY SOMEONE WHO ISN'T TIGER TRIBE.
HOW DO WE KNOW WE CAN TRUST DUNCAN?
SIGH
PERHAPS BECAUSE HE HAS NOW SAVED YOUR LIFE ON MULTIPLE OCCASIONS?
I'M GONNA HAVE TO TAKE A RAIN CHECK ON THIS CONVERSATION. UGH, RAIN . . .
FINALLY!
CLICK

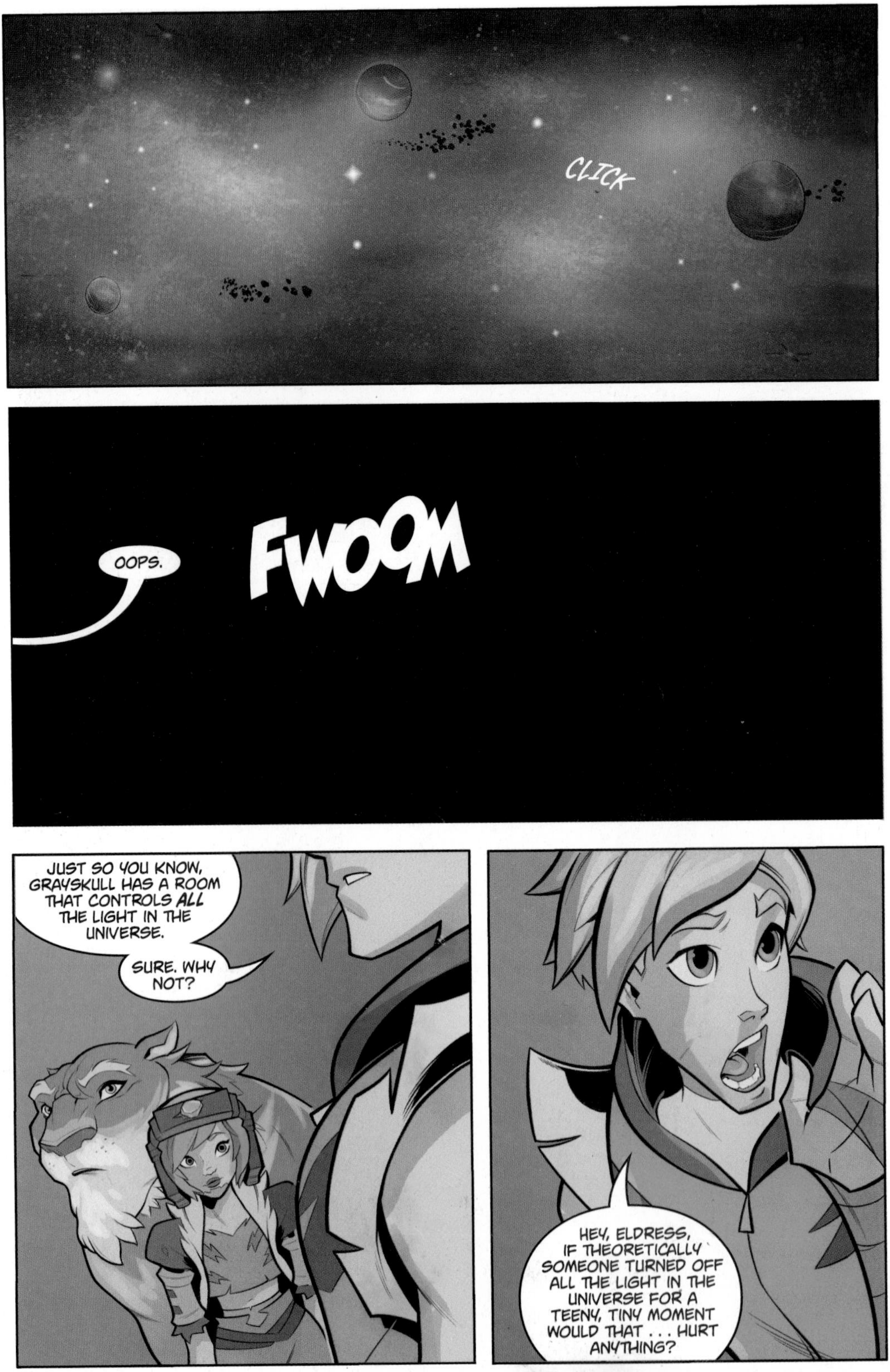
CLICK
OOPS.
FWOOM
JUST SO YOU KNOW, GRAYSKULL HAS A ROOM THAT CONTROLS ***ALL*** THE LIGHT IN THE UNIVERSE.
SURE. WHY NOT?
HEY, ELDRESS, IF THEORETICALLY SOMEONE TURNED OFF ALL THE LIGHT IN THE UNIVERSE FOR A TEENY, TINY MOMENT WOULD THAT . . . HURT ANYTHING?

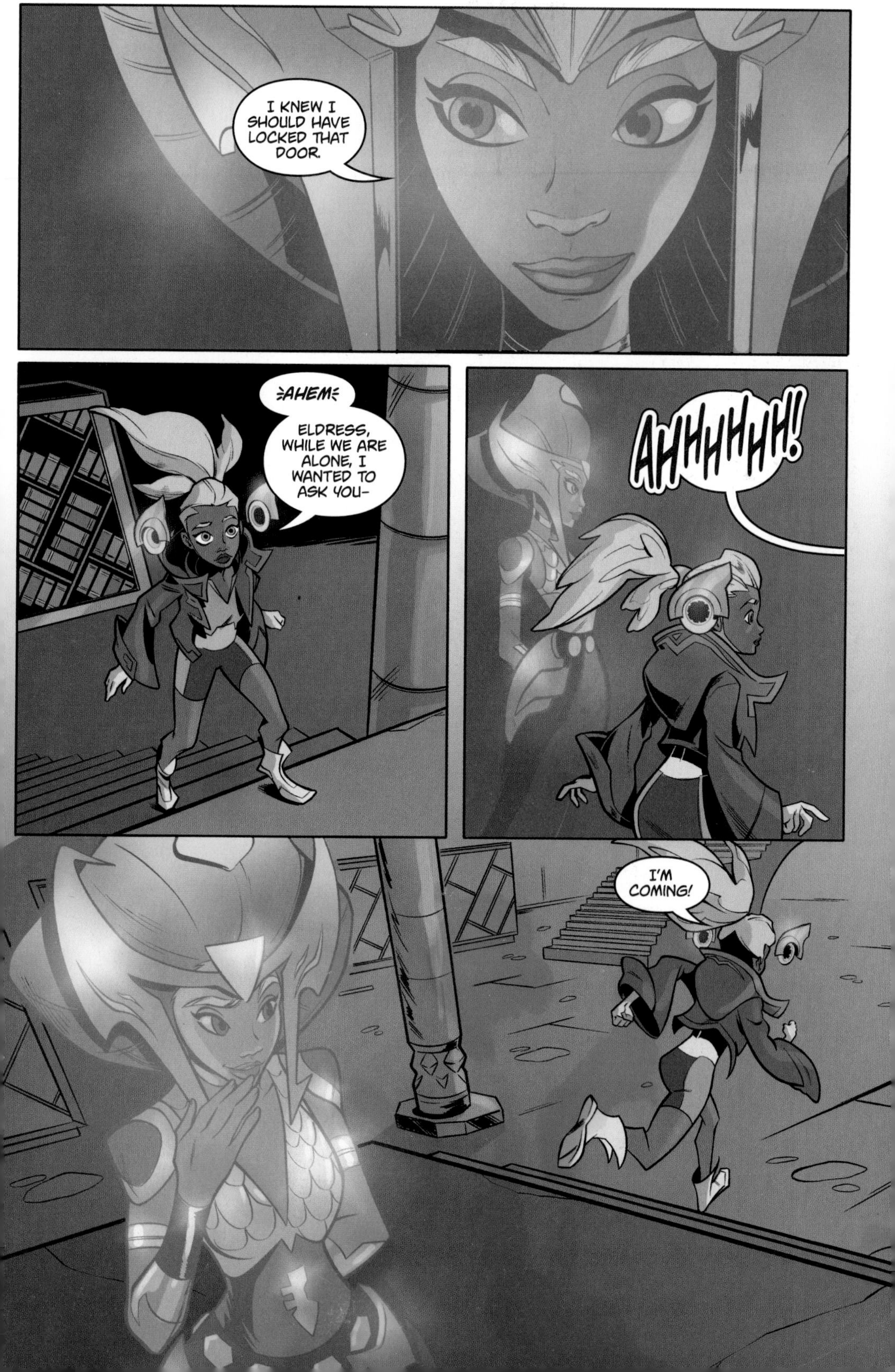
I KNEW I SHOULD HAVE LOCKED THAT DOOR.
AHEM
ELDRESS, WHILE WE ARE ALONE, I WANTED TO ASK YOU-
AHHHHHH!
I'M COMING!

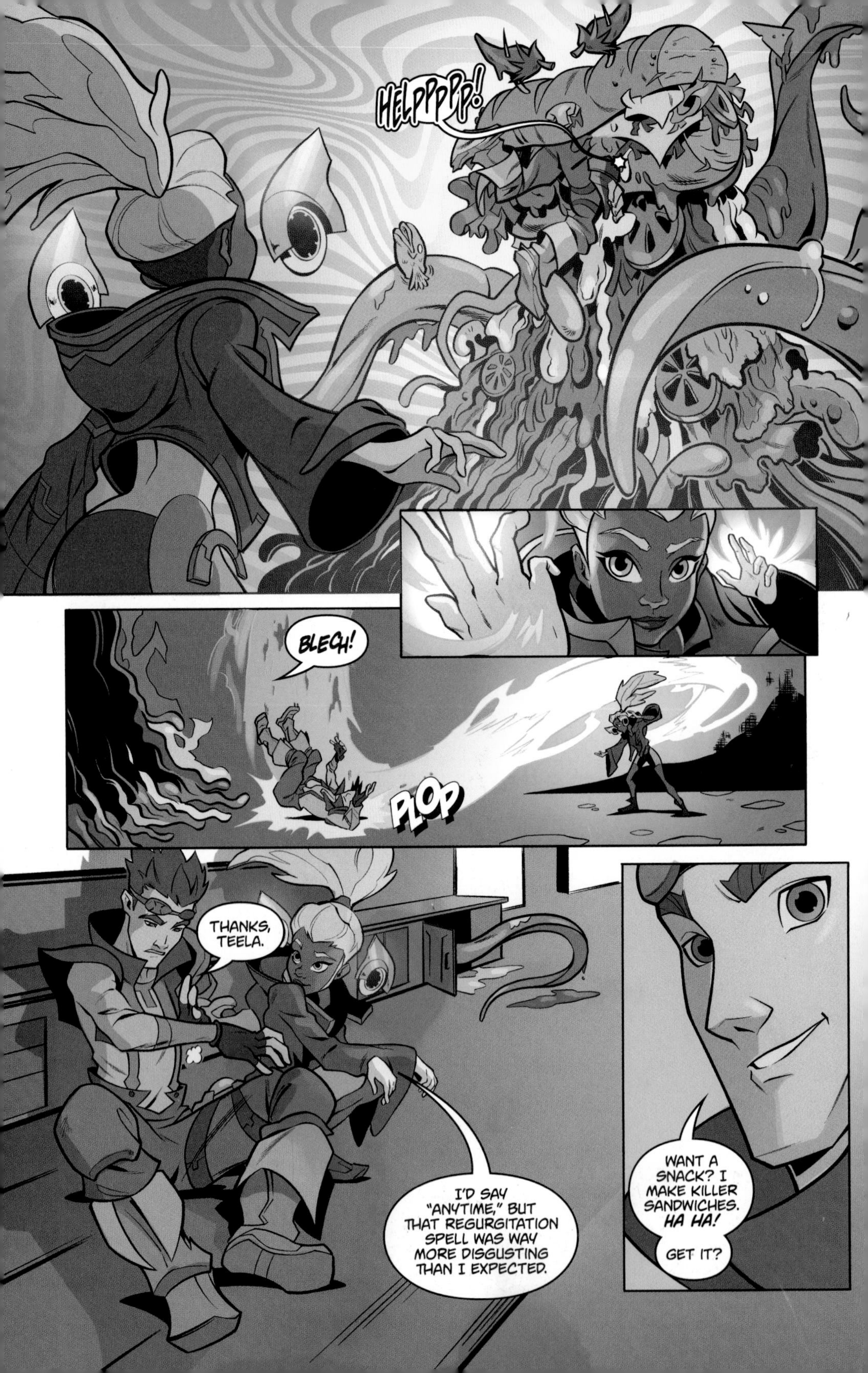
HELPPPPP!
BLECH!
PLOP
THANKS, TEELA.
I'D SAY "ANYTIME," BUT THAT REGURGITATION SPELL WAS WAY MORE DISGUSTING THAN I EXPECTED.
WANT A SNACK? I MAKE KILLER SANDWICHES. HA HA!
GET IT?

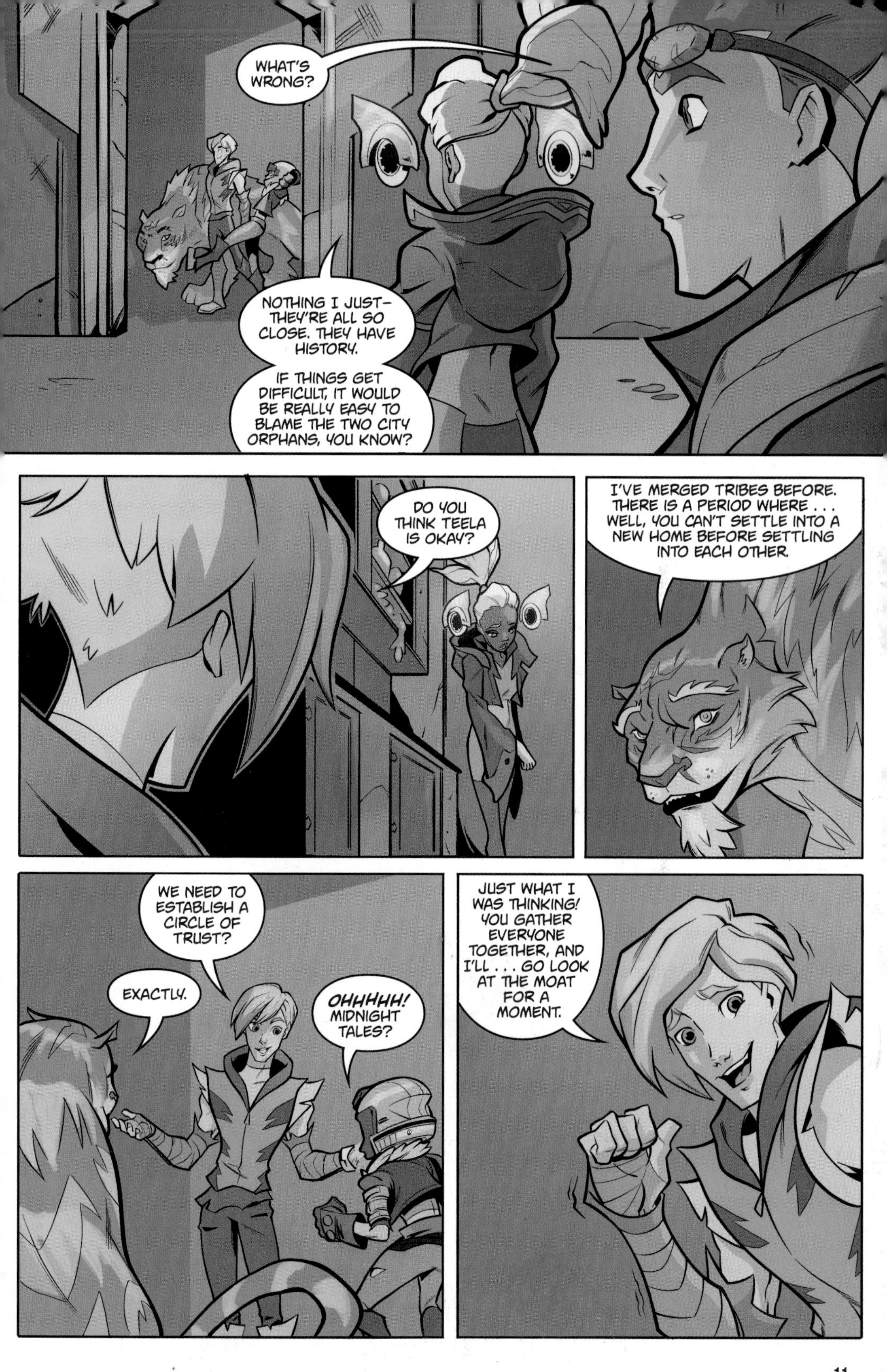
WHAT'S WRONG?
NOTHING I JUST— THEY'RE ALL SO CLOSE. THEY HAVE HISTORY.
IF THINGS GET DIFFICULT, IT WOULD BE REALLY EASY TO BLAME THE TWO CITY ORPHANS, YOU KNOW?
DO YOU THINK TEELA IS OKAY?
I'VE MERGED TRIBES BEFORE. THERE IS A PERIOD WHERE . . . WELL, YOU CAN'T SETTLE INTO A NEW HOME BEFORE SETTLING INTO EACH OTHER.
WE NEED TO ESTABLISH A CIRCLE OF TRUST?
EXACTLY.
OHHHHH! MIDNIGHT TALES?
JUST WHAT I WAS THINKING! YOU GATHER EVERYONE TOGETHER, AND I'LL . . . GO LOOK AT THE MOAT FOR A MOMENT.

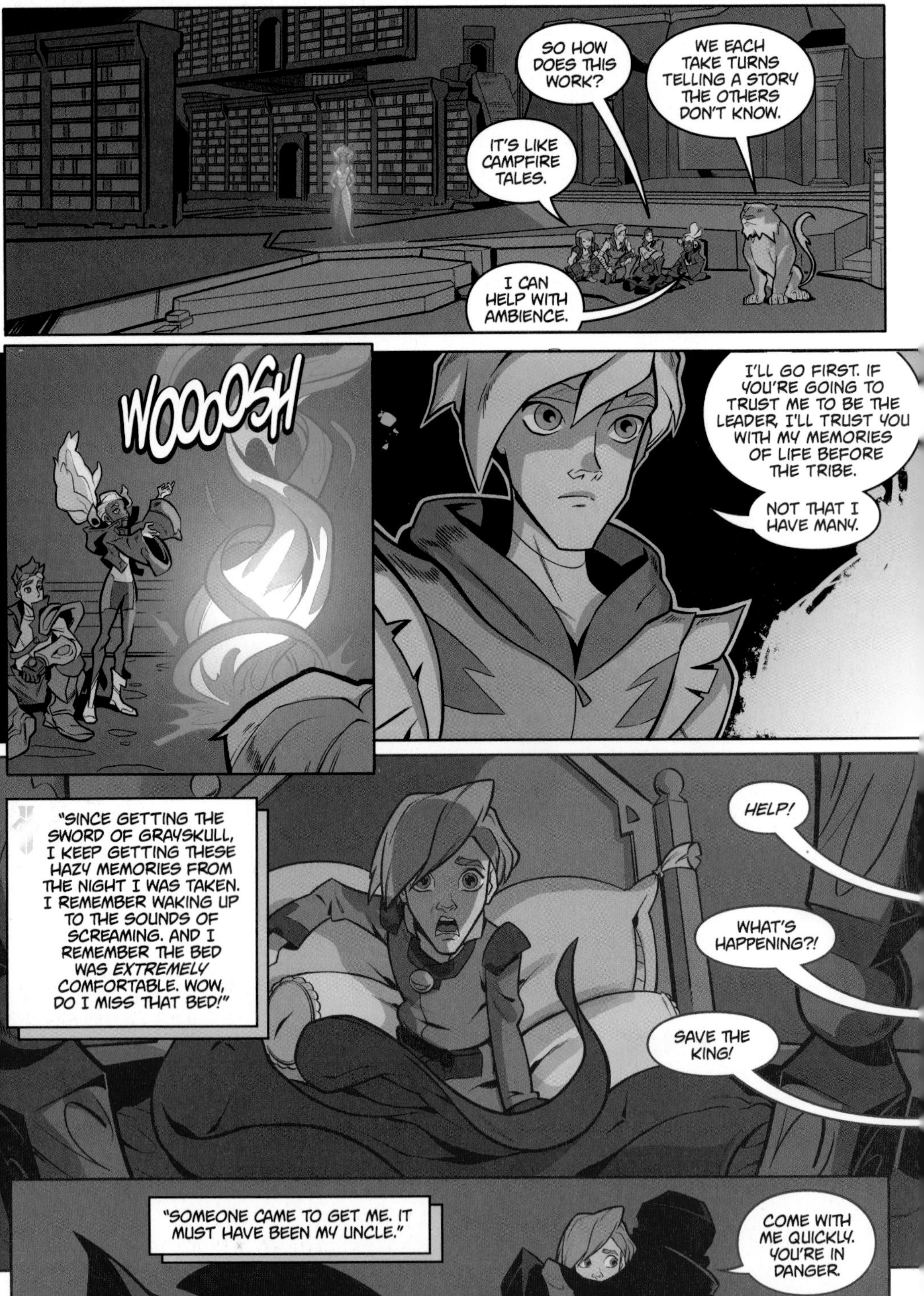
SO HOW DOES THIS WORK?
WE EACH TAKE TURNS TELLING A STORY THE OTHERS DON'T KNOW.
IT'S LIKE CAMPFIRE TALES.
I CAN HELP WITH AMBIENCE.
WOOOOSH
I'LL GO FIRST. IF YOU'RE GOING TO TRUST ME TO BE THE LEADER, I'LL TRUST YOU WITH MY MEMORIES OF LIFE BEFORE THE TRIBE.
NOT THAT I HAVE MANY.
"SINCE GETTING THE SWORD OF GRAYSKULL, I KEEP GETTING THESE HAZY MEMORIES FROM THE NIGHT I WAS TAKEN. I REMEMBER WAKING UP TO THE SOUNDS OF SCREAMING. AND I REMEMBER THE BED WAS *EXTREMELY* COMFORTABLE. WOW, DO I MISS THAT BED!"
HELP!
WHAT'S HAPPENING?!
SAVE THE KING!
"SOMEONE CAME TO GET ME. IT MUST HAVE BEEN MY UNCLE."
COME WITH ME QUICKLY. YOU'RE IN DANGER.

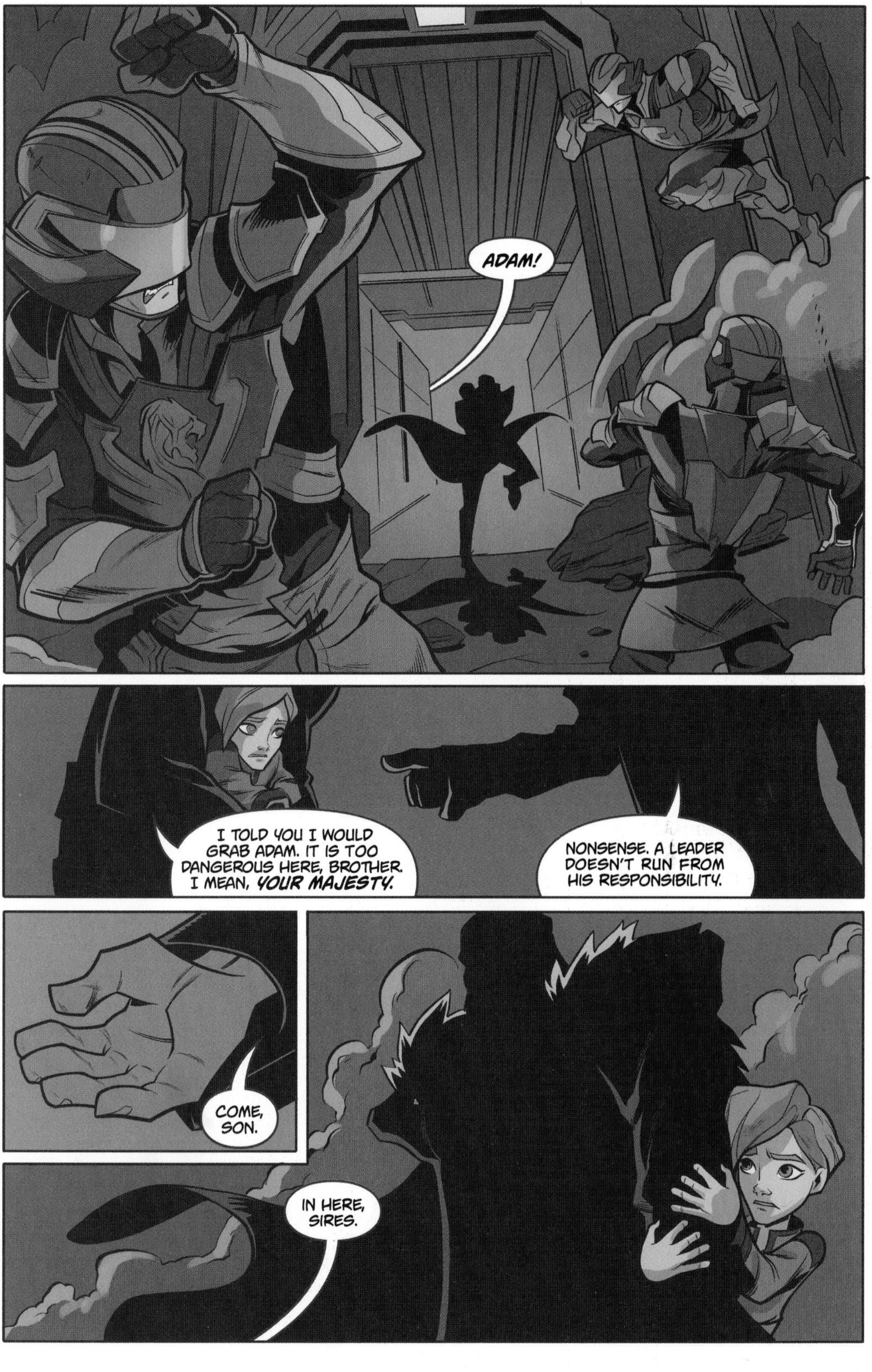
ADAM!
I TOLD YOU I WOULD GRAB ADAM. IT IS TOO DANGEROUS HERE, BROTHER. I MEAN, YOUR MAJESTY.
NONSENSE. A LEADER DOESN'T RUN FROM HIS RESPONSIBILITY.
COME, SON.
IN HERE, SIRES.

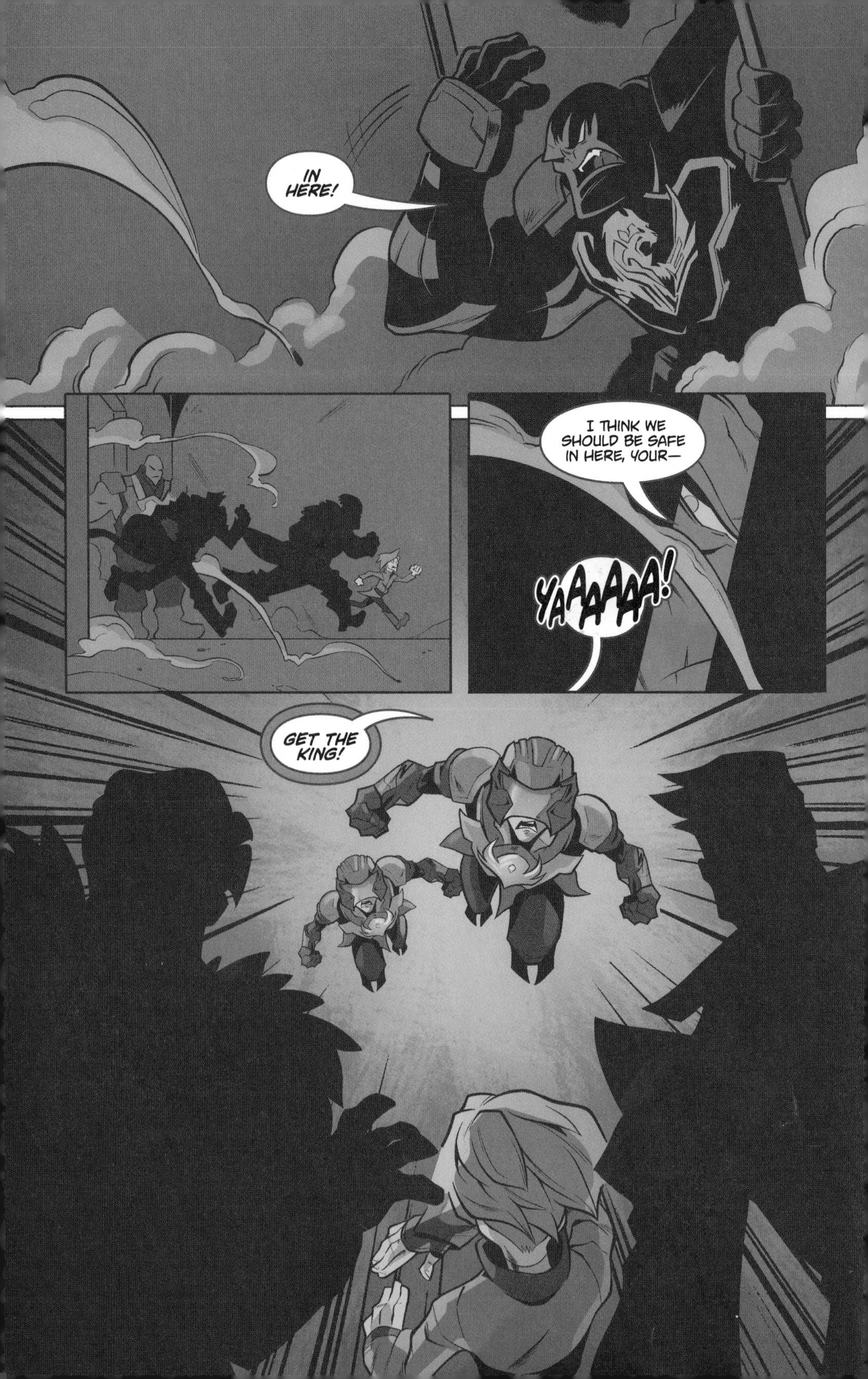
IN HERE!
I THINK WE SHOULD BE SAFE IN HERE, YOUR—
YAAAAAA!
GET THE KING!

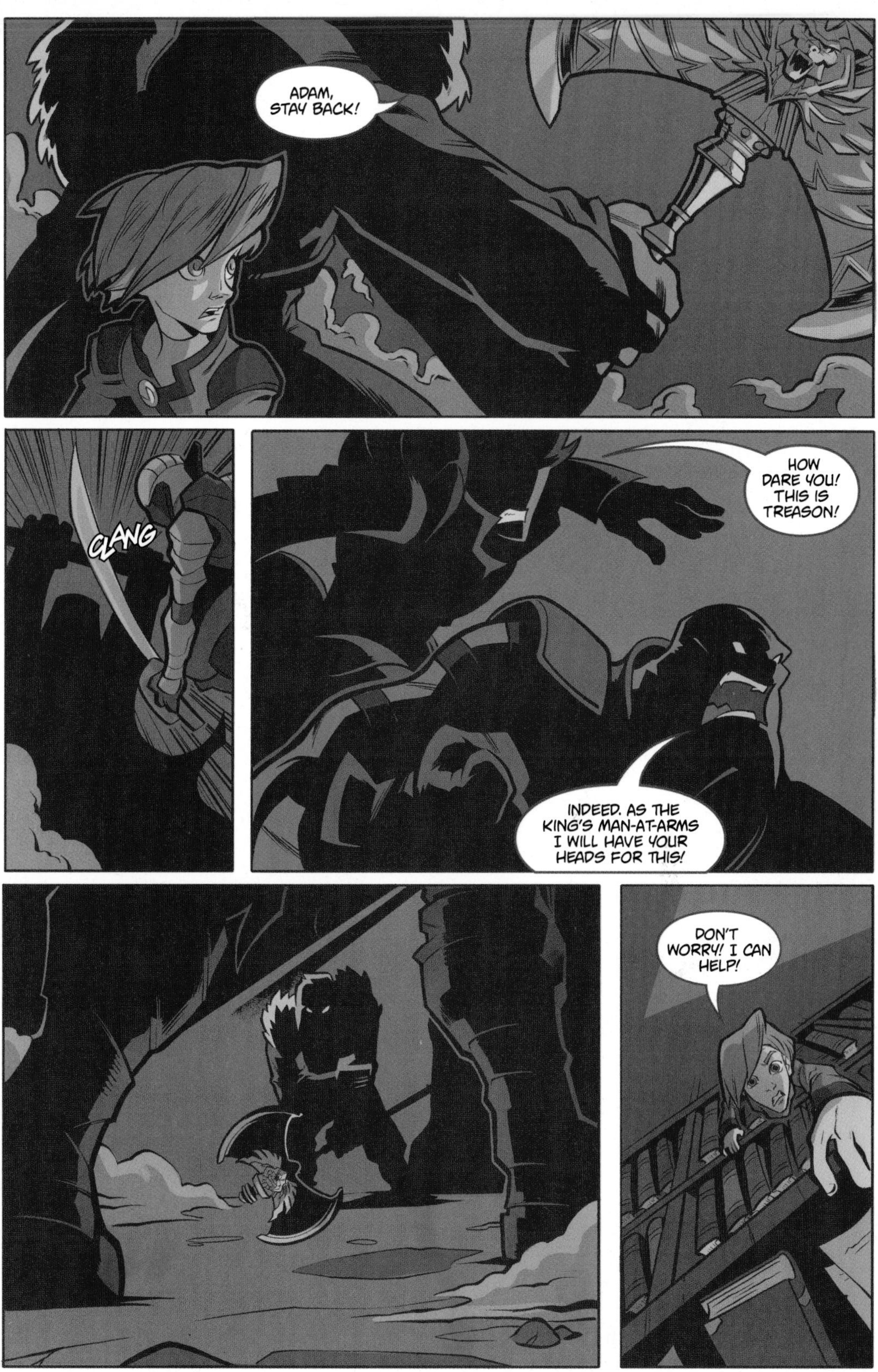
ADAM, STAY BACK!
CLANG
HOW DARE YOU! THIS IS TREASON!
INDEED. AS THE KING'S MAN-AT-ARMS I WILL HAVE YOUR HEADS FOR THIS!
DON'T WORRY! I CAN HELP!

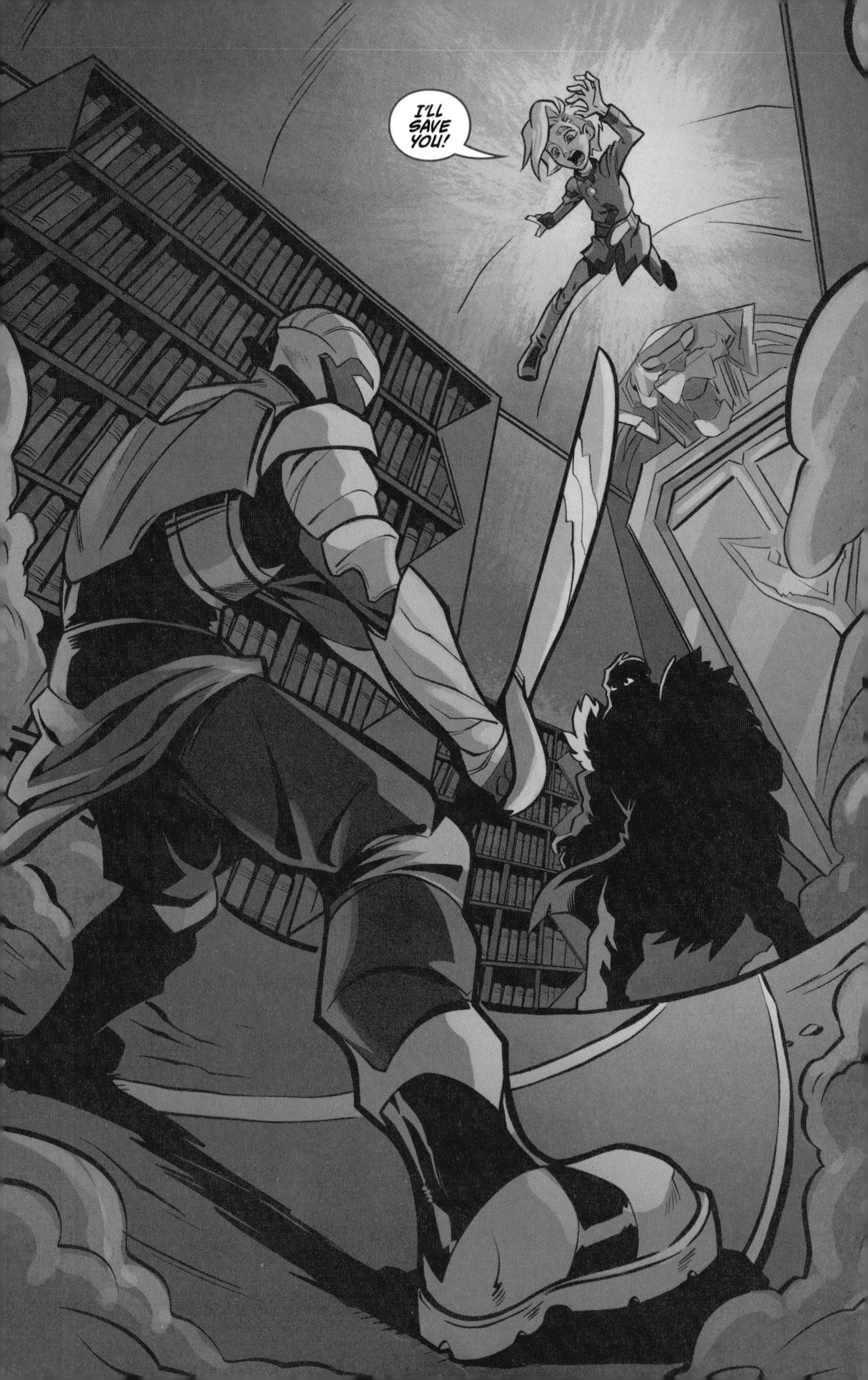
I'LL SAVE YOU!

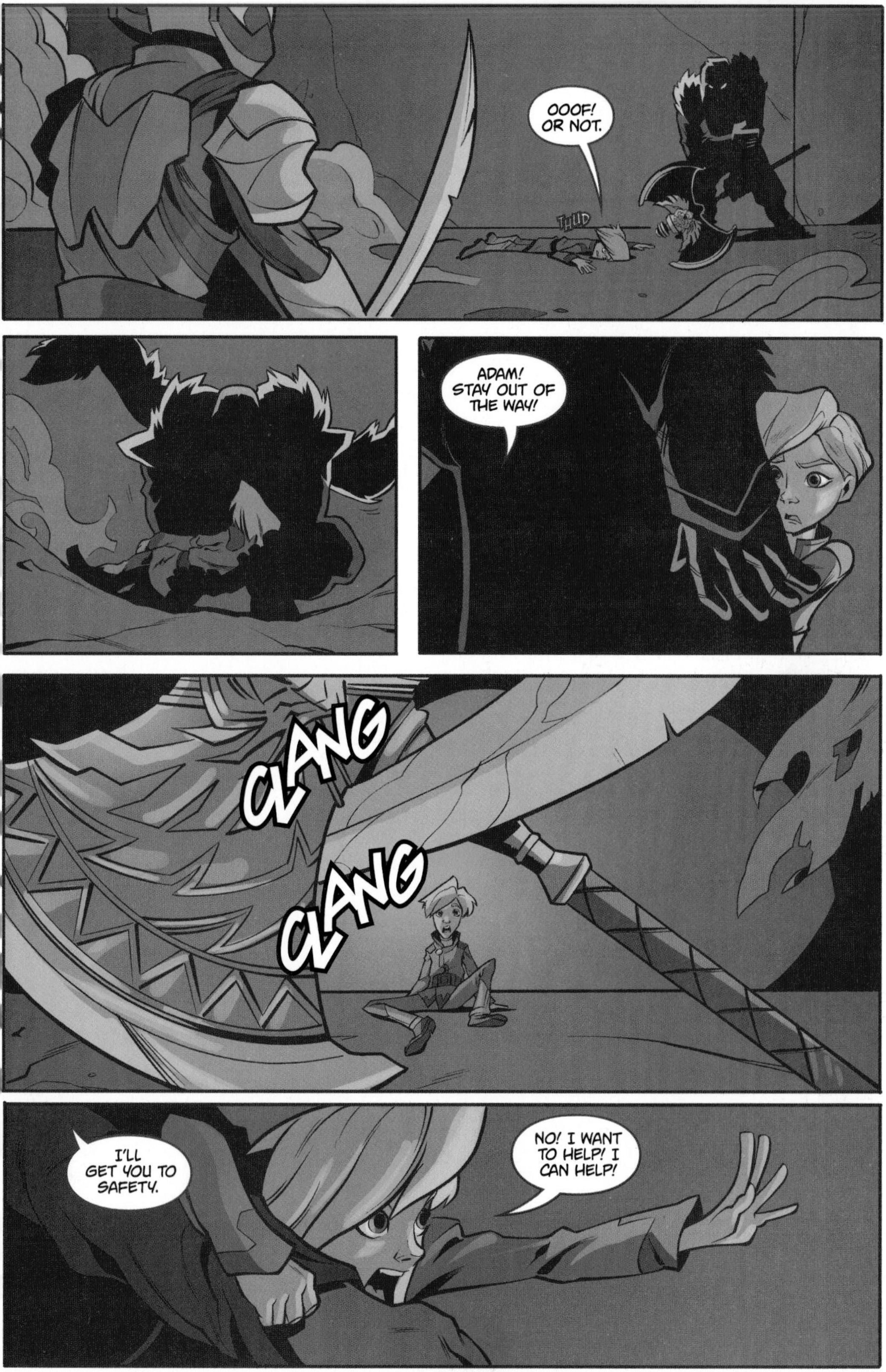
OOOF! OR NOT.
THUD
ADAM! STAY OUT OF THE WAY!
CLANG
CLANG
I'LL GET YOU TO SAFETY.
NO! I WANT TO HELP! I CAN HELP!

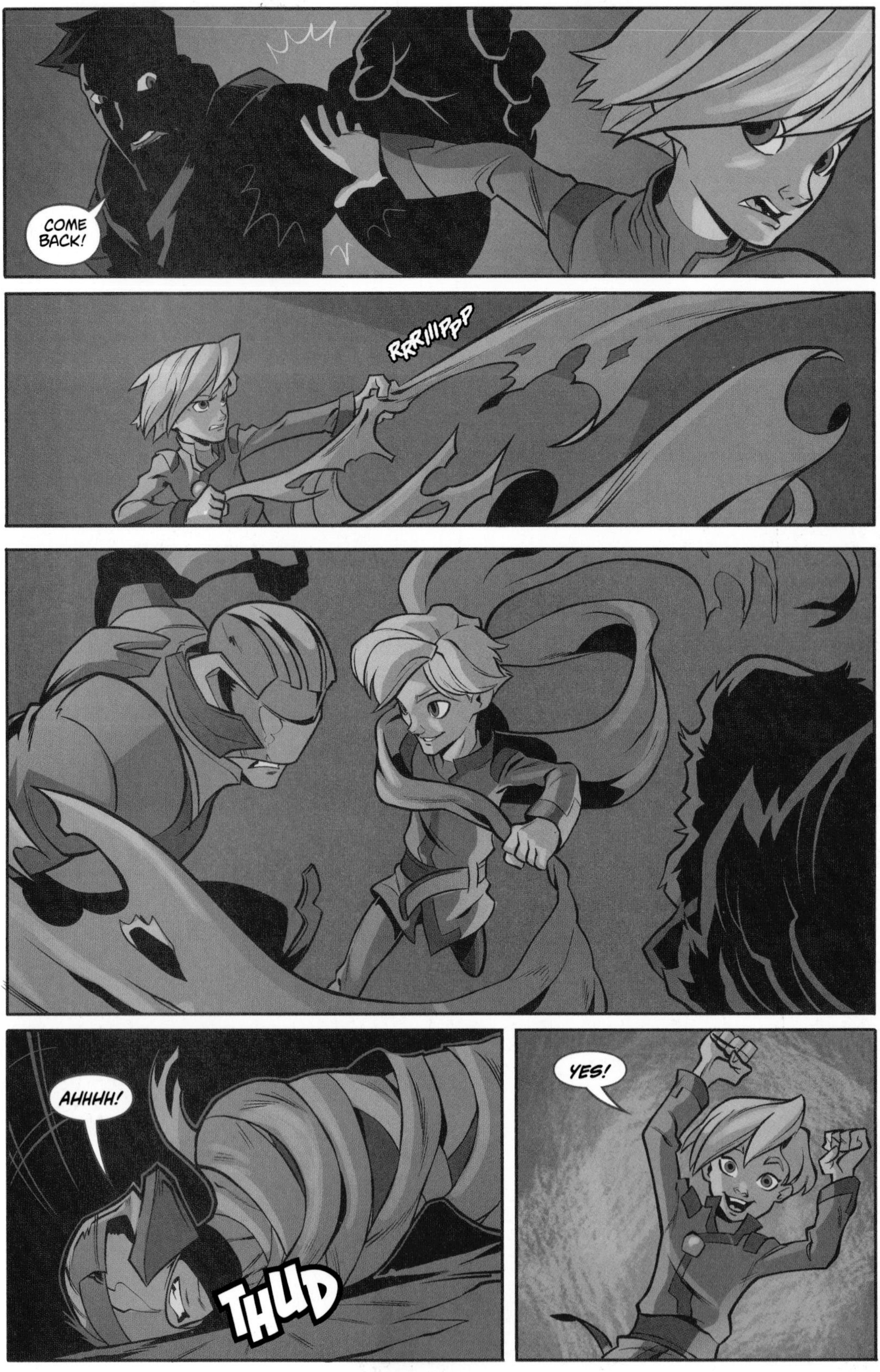
COME BACK!
RRRIIIPPP
AHHHH!
THUD
YES!

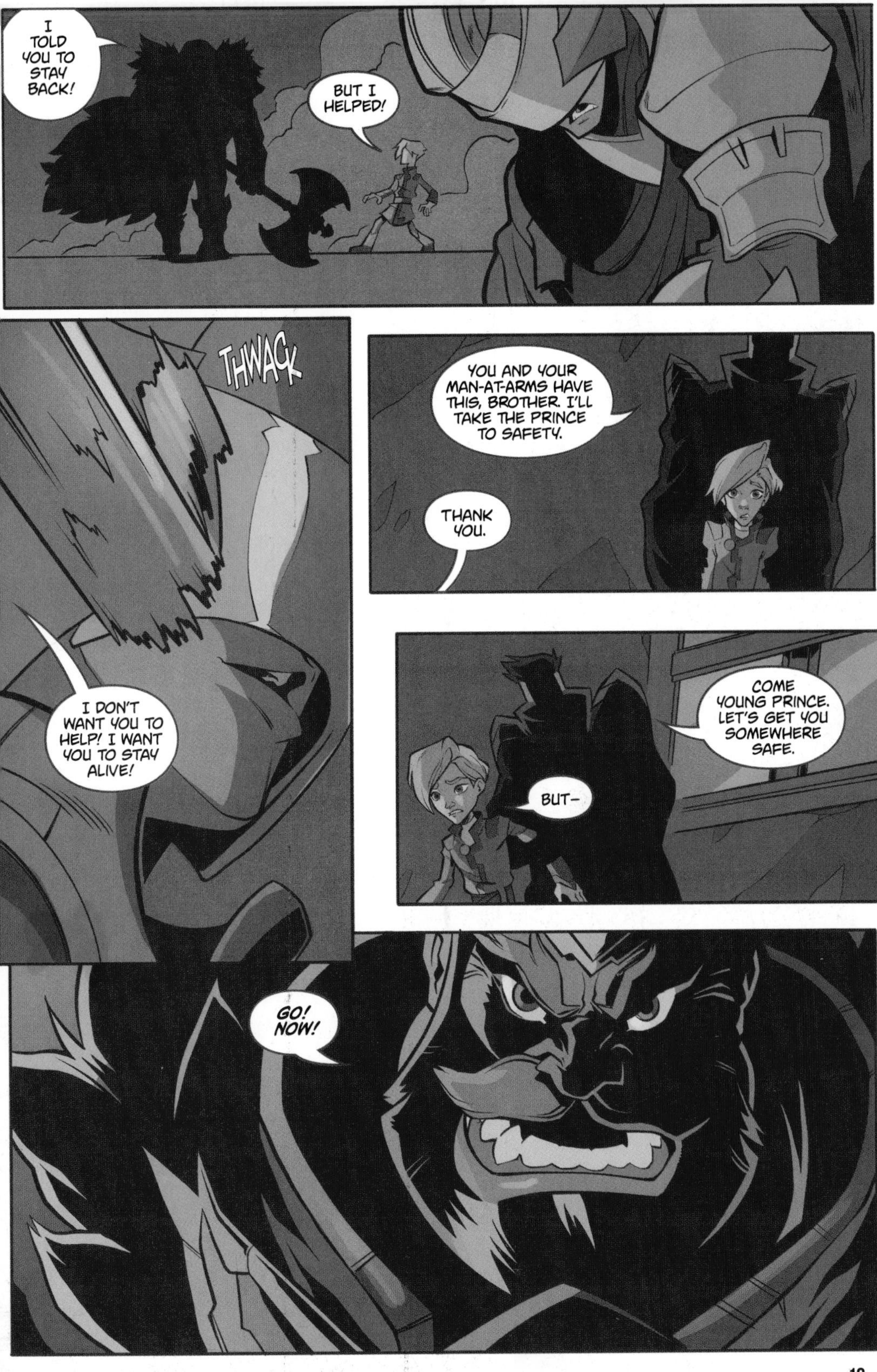
I TOLD YOU TO STAY BACK!
BUT I HELPED!
THWACK
I DON'T WANT YOU TO HELP! I WANT YOU TO STAY ALIVE!
YOU AND YOUR MAN-AT-ARMS HAVE THIS, BROTHER. I'LL TAKE THE PRINCE TO SAFETY.
THANK YOU.
COME YOUNG PRINCE. LET'S GET YOU SOMEWHERE SAFE.
BUT–
GO! NOW!

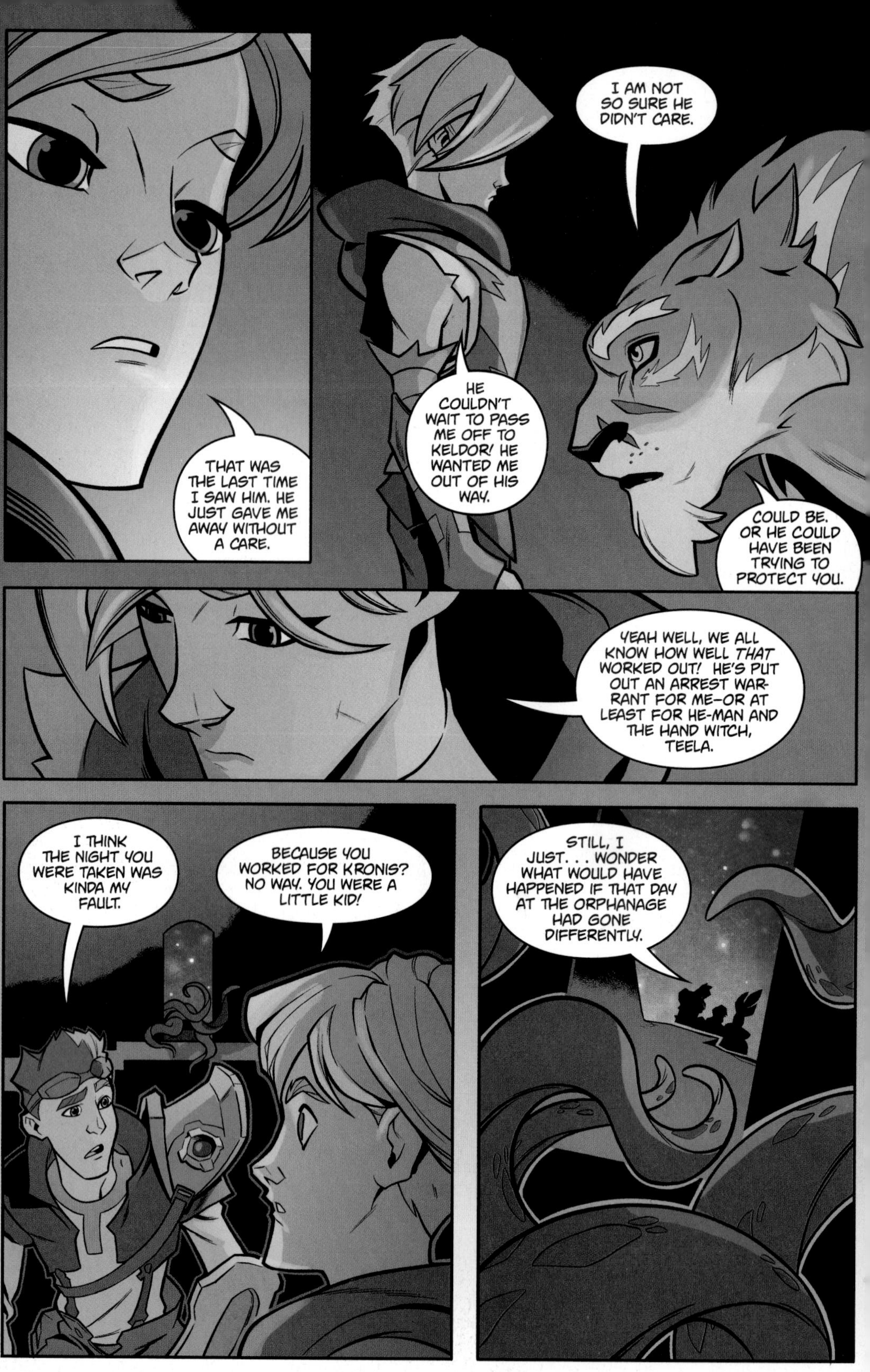
THAT WAS THE LAST TIME I SAW HIM. HE JUST GAVE ME AWAY WITHOUT A CARE.
HE COULDN'T WAIT TO PASS ME OFF TO KELDOR! HE WANTED ME OUT OF HIS WAY.
I AM NOT SO SURE HE DIDN'T CARE.
COULD BE. OR HE COULD HAVE BEEN TRYING TO PROTECT YOU.
YEAH WELL, WE ALL KNOW HOW WELL *THAT* WORKED OUT! HE'S PUT OUT AN ARREST WAR-RANT FOR ME–OR AT LEAST FOR HE-MAN AND THE HAND WITCH, TEELA.
I THINK THE NIGHT YOU WERE TAKEN WAS KINDA MY FAULT.
BECAUSE YOU WORKED FOR KRONIS? NO WAY. YOU WERE A LITTLE KID!
STILL, I JUST. . . WONDER WHAT WOULD HAVE HAPPENED IF THAT DAY AT THE ORPHANAGE HAD GONE DIFFERENTLY.

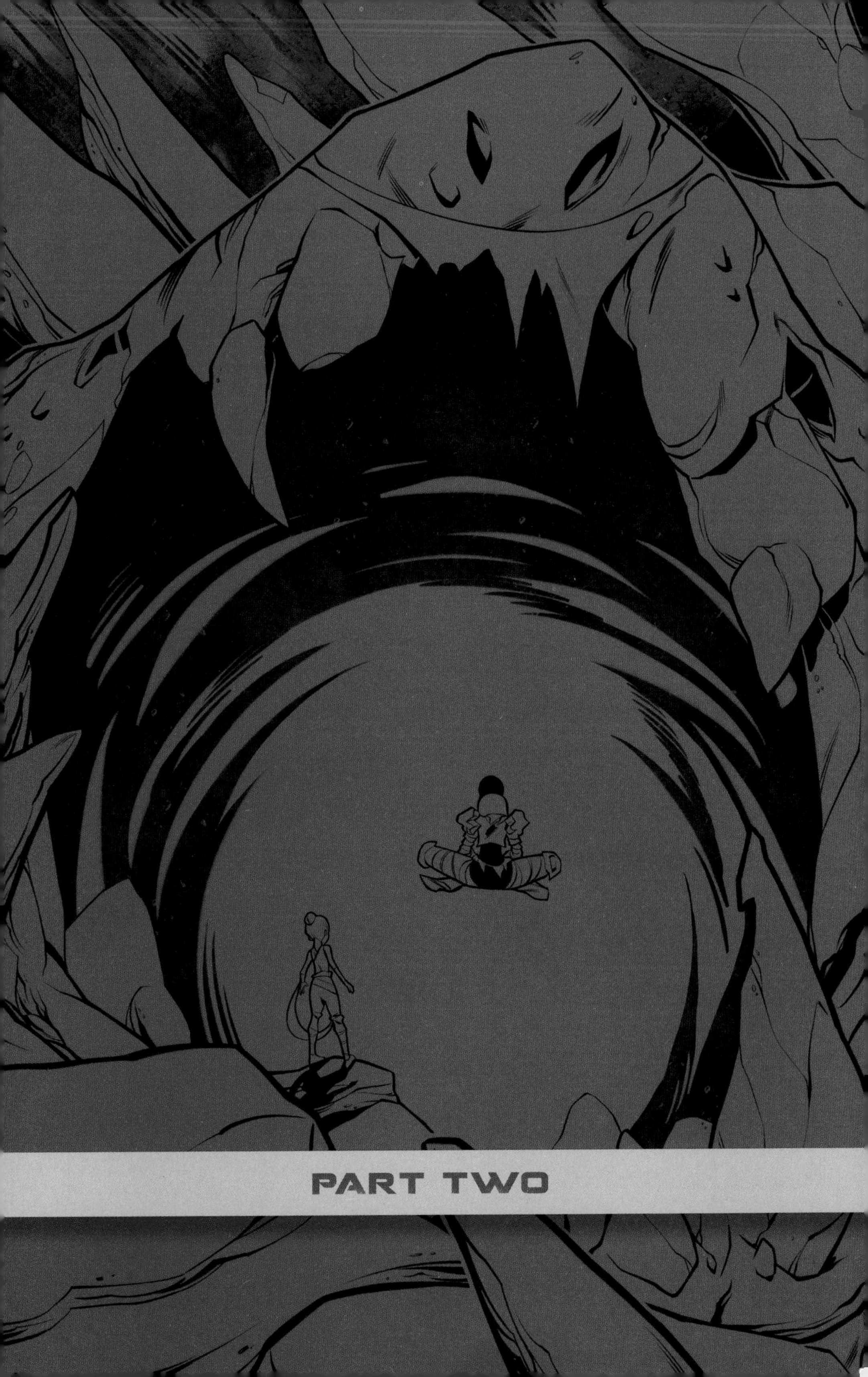

PART TWO

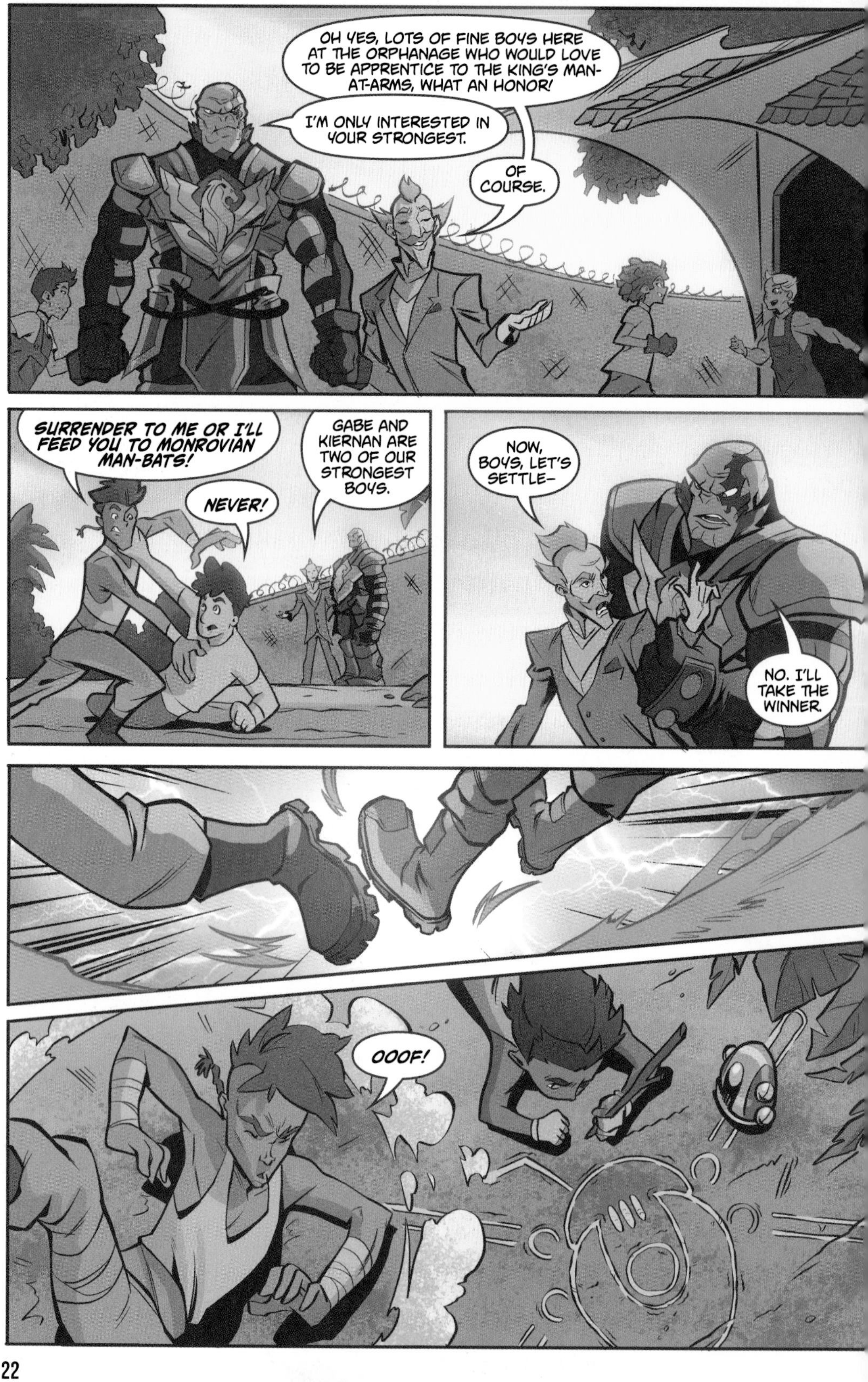
OH YES, LOTS OF FINE BOYS HERE AT THE ORPHANAGE WHO WOULD LOVE TO BE APPRENTICE TO THE KING'S MAN-AT-ARMS, WHAT AN HONOR!
I'M ONLY INTERESTED IN YOUR STRONGEST.
OF COURSE.
SURRENDER TO ME OR I'LL FEED YOU TO MONROVIAN MAN-BATS!
NEVER!
GABE AND KIERNAN ARE TWO OF OUR STRONGEST BOYS.
NOW, BOYS, LET'S SETTLE-
NO. I'LL TAKE THE WINNER.
OOOF!

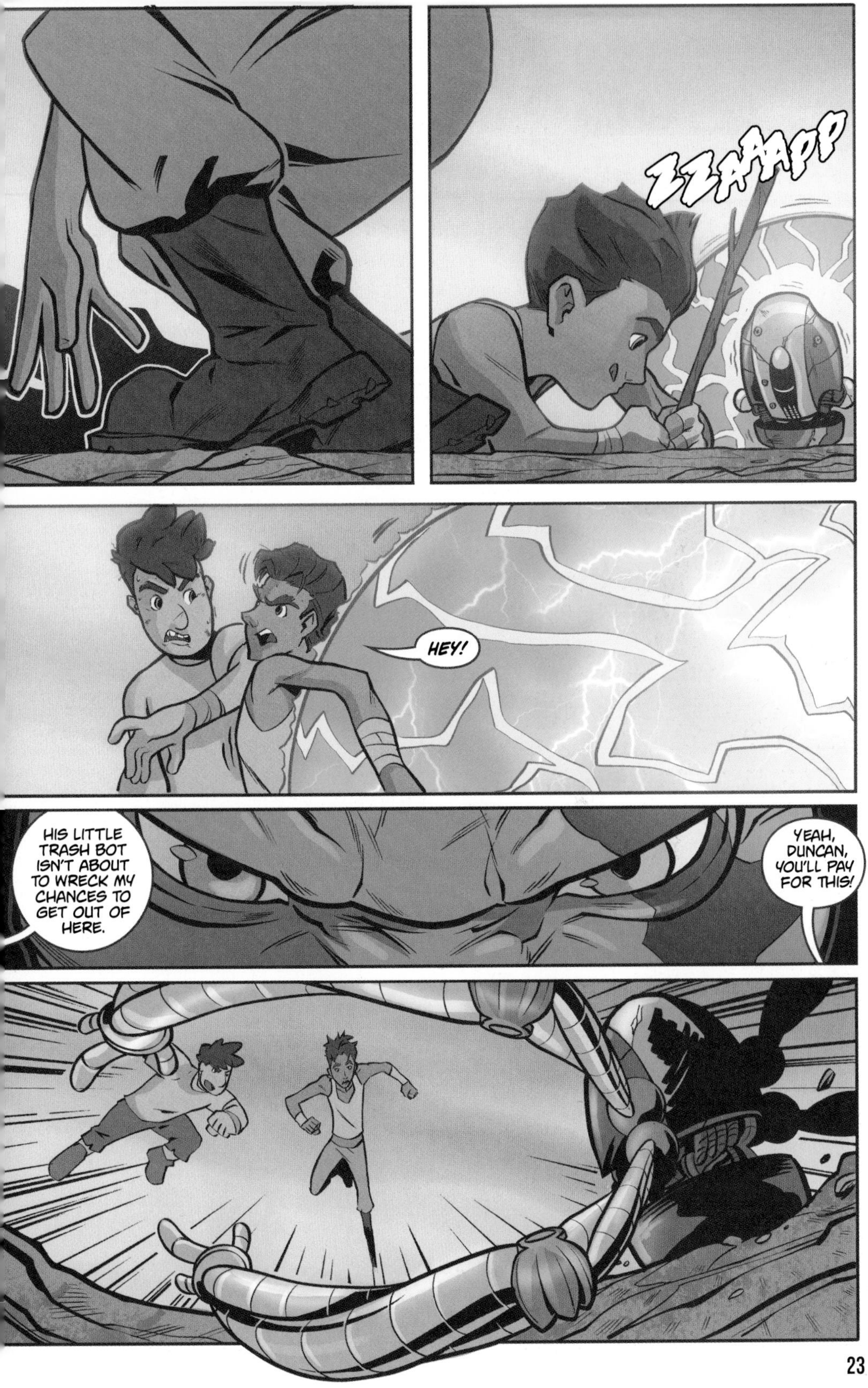
ZZAAAAPP
HEY!
HIS LITTLE TRASH BOT ISN'T ABOUT TO WRECK MY CHANCES TO GET OUT OF HERE.
YEAH, DUNCAN, YOU'LL PAY FOR THIS!

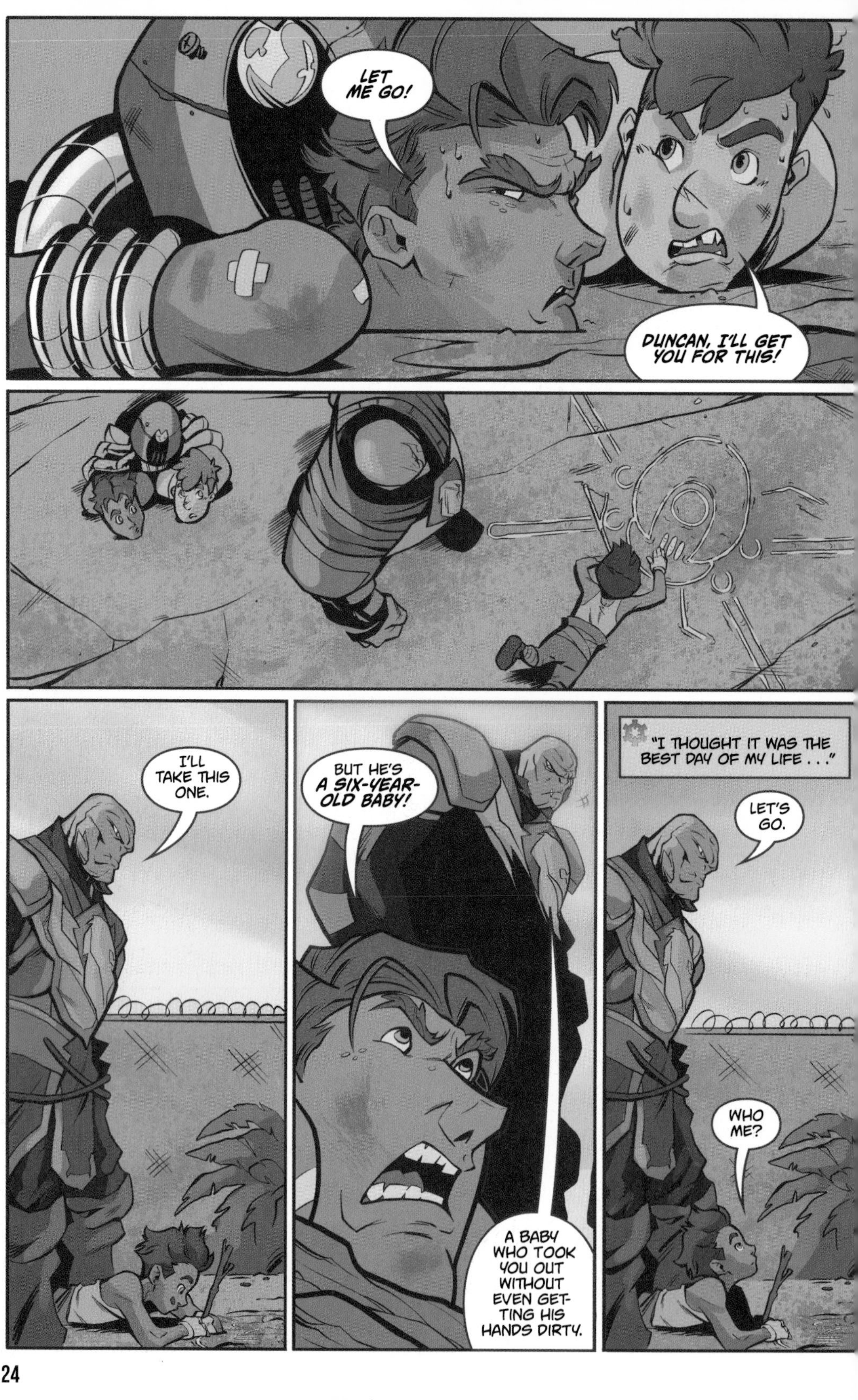
LET ME GO!
DUNCAN, I'LL GET YOU FOR THIS!
I'LL TAKE THIS ONE.
BUT HE'S A SIX-YEAR-OLD BABY!
A BABY WHO TOOK YOU OUT WITHOUT EVEN GET-TING HIS HANDS DIRTY.
"I THOUGHT IT WAS THE BEST DAY OF MY LIFE . . ."
LET'S GO.
WHO ME?

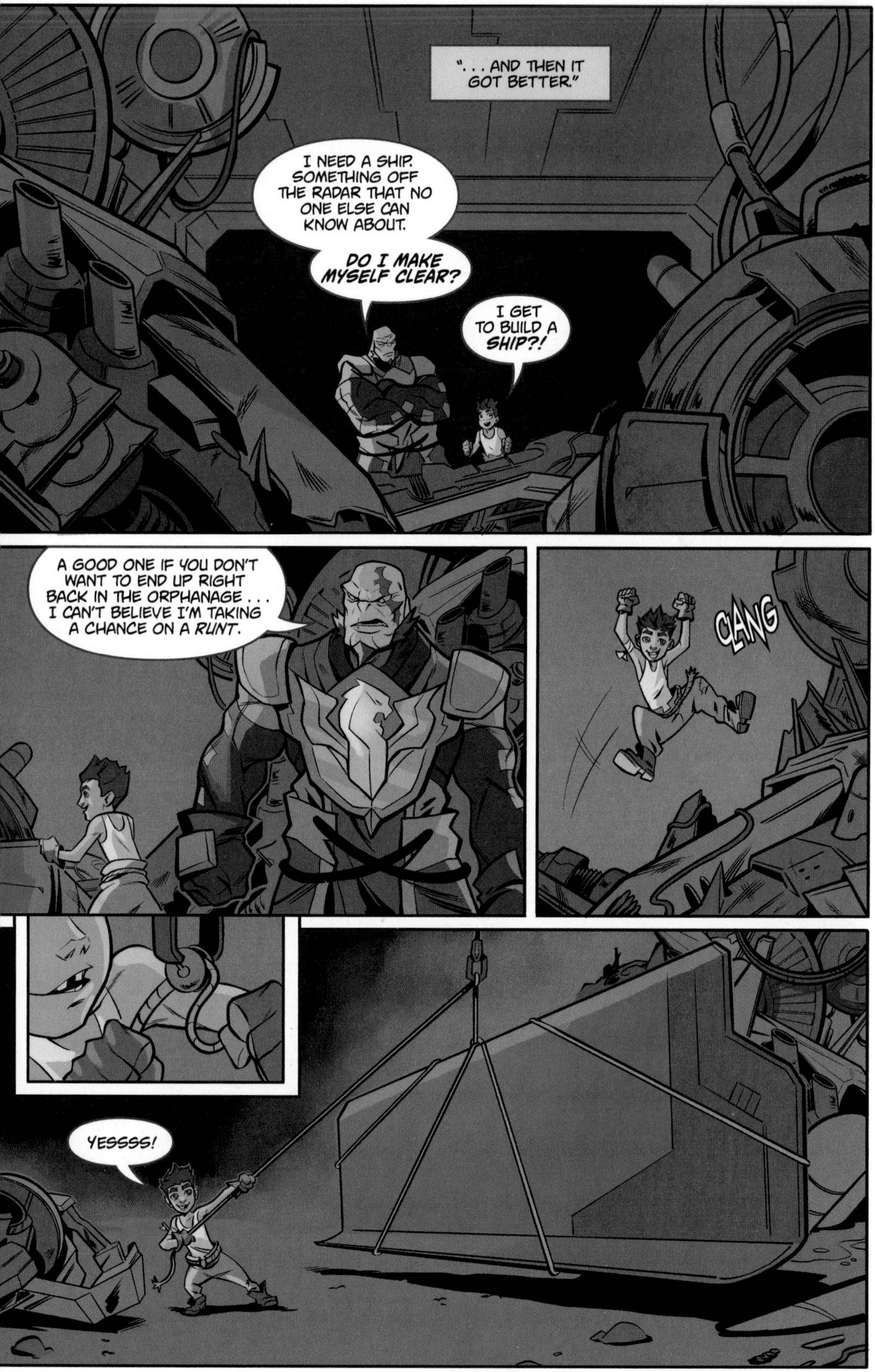
". . . AND THEN IT GOT BETTER."
I NEED A SHIP. SOMETHING OFF THE RADAR THAT NO ONE ELSE CAN KNOW ABOUT.
DO I MAKE MYSELF CLEAR?
I GET TO BUILD A SHIP?!
A GOOD ONE IF YOU DON'T WANT TO END UP RIGHT BACK IN THE ORPHANAGE . . . I CAN'T BELIEVE I'M TAKING A CHANCE ON A RUNT.
CLANG
YESSSS!

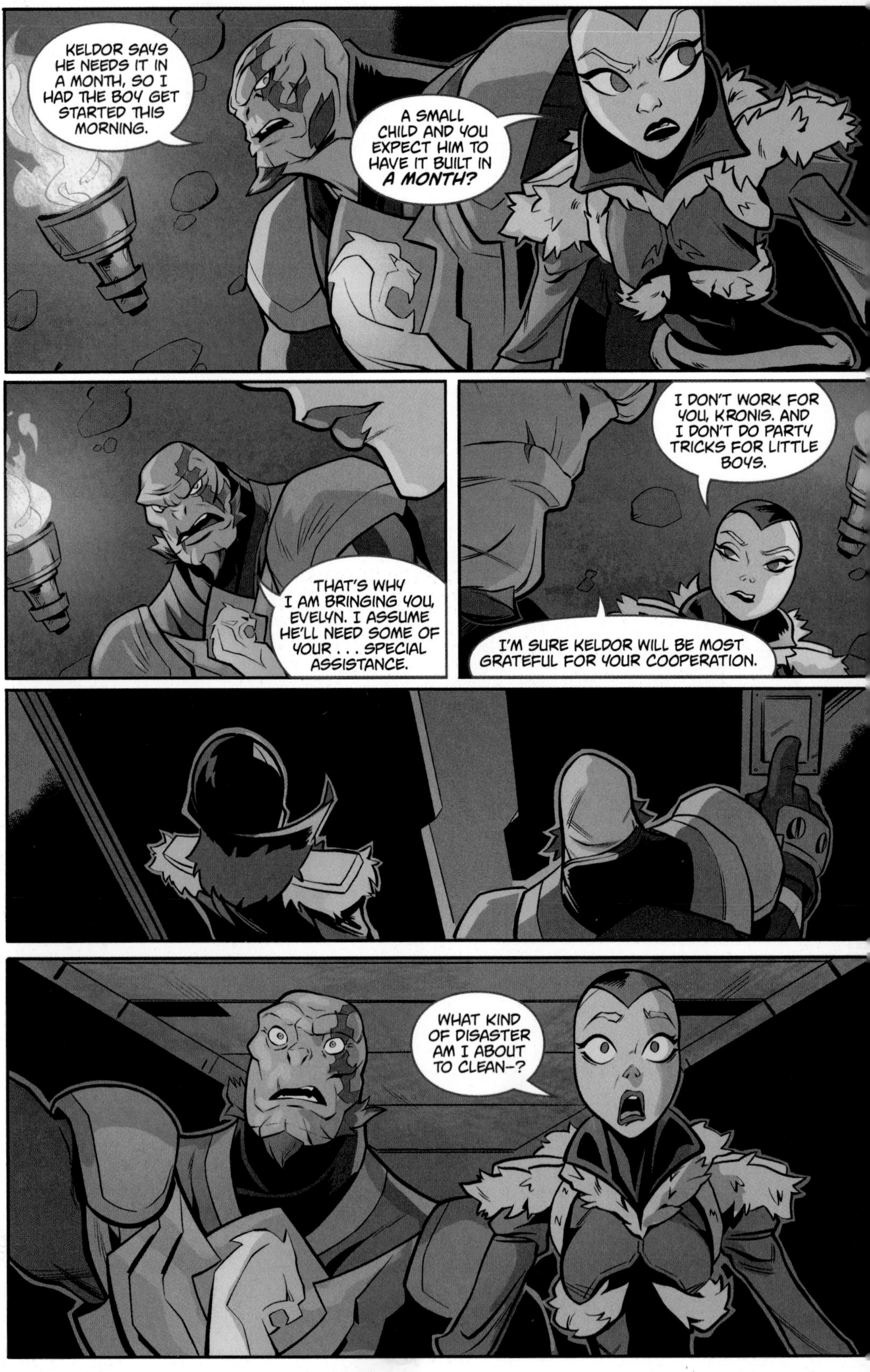
KELDOR SAYS HE NEEDS IT IN A MONTH, SO I HAD THE BOY GET STARTED THIS MORNING.
A SMALL CHILD AND YOU EXPECT HIM TO HAVE IT BUILT IN *A MONTH?*
THAT'S WHY I AM BRINGING YOU, EVELYN. I ASSUME HE'LL NEED SOME OF YOUR . . . SPECIAL ASSISTANCE.
I DON'T WORK FOR YOU, KRONIS. AND I DON'T DO PARTY TRICKS FOR LITTLE BOYS.
I'M SURE KELDOR WILL BE MOST GRATEFUL FOR YOUR COOPERATION.
WHAT KIND OF DISASTER AM I ABOUT TO CLEAN-?

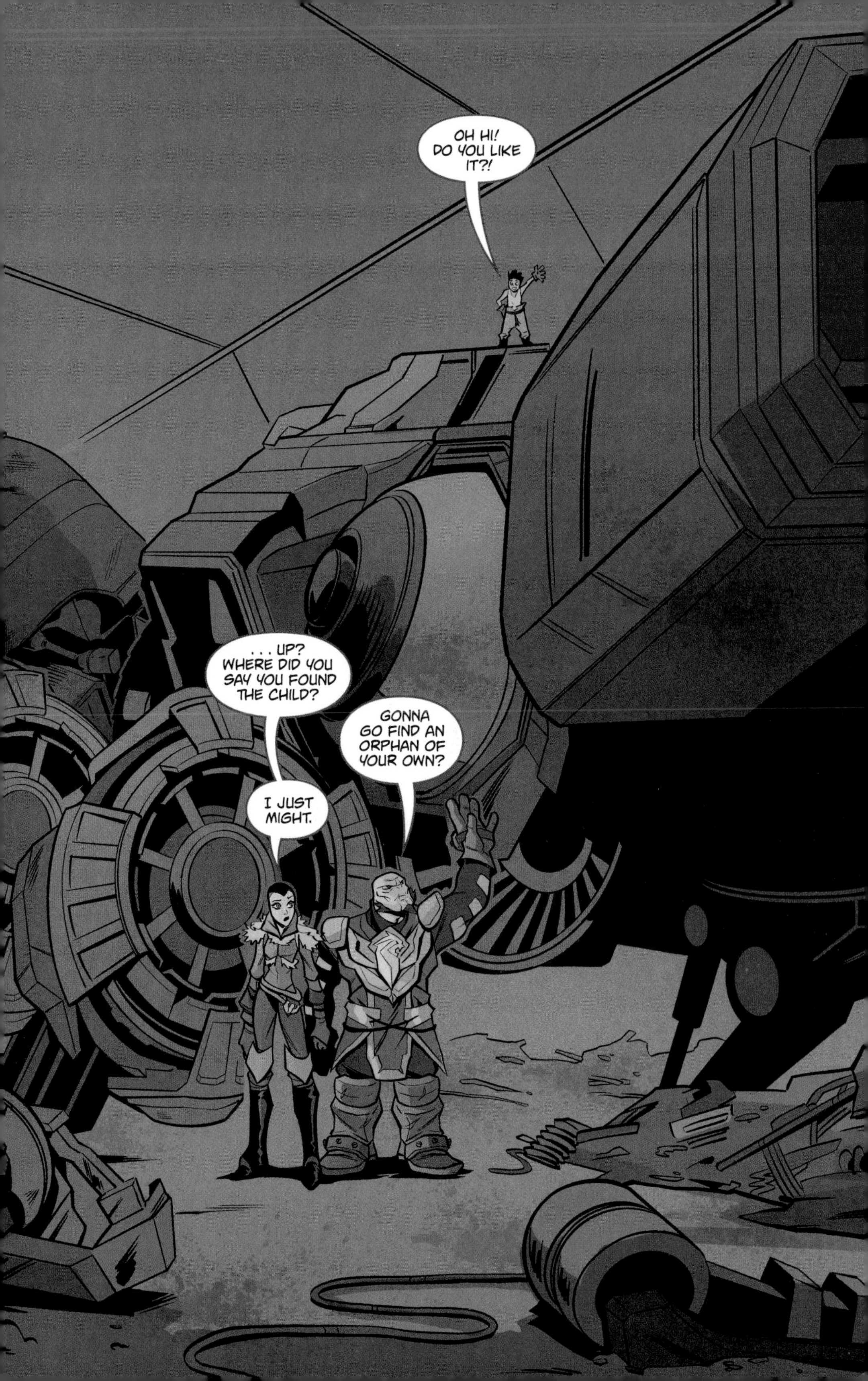
OH HI! DO YOU LIKE IT?!
. . . UP? WHERE DID YOU SAY YOU FOUND THE CHILD?
GONNA GO FIND AN ORPHAN OF YOUR OWN?
I JUST MIGHT.

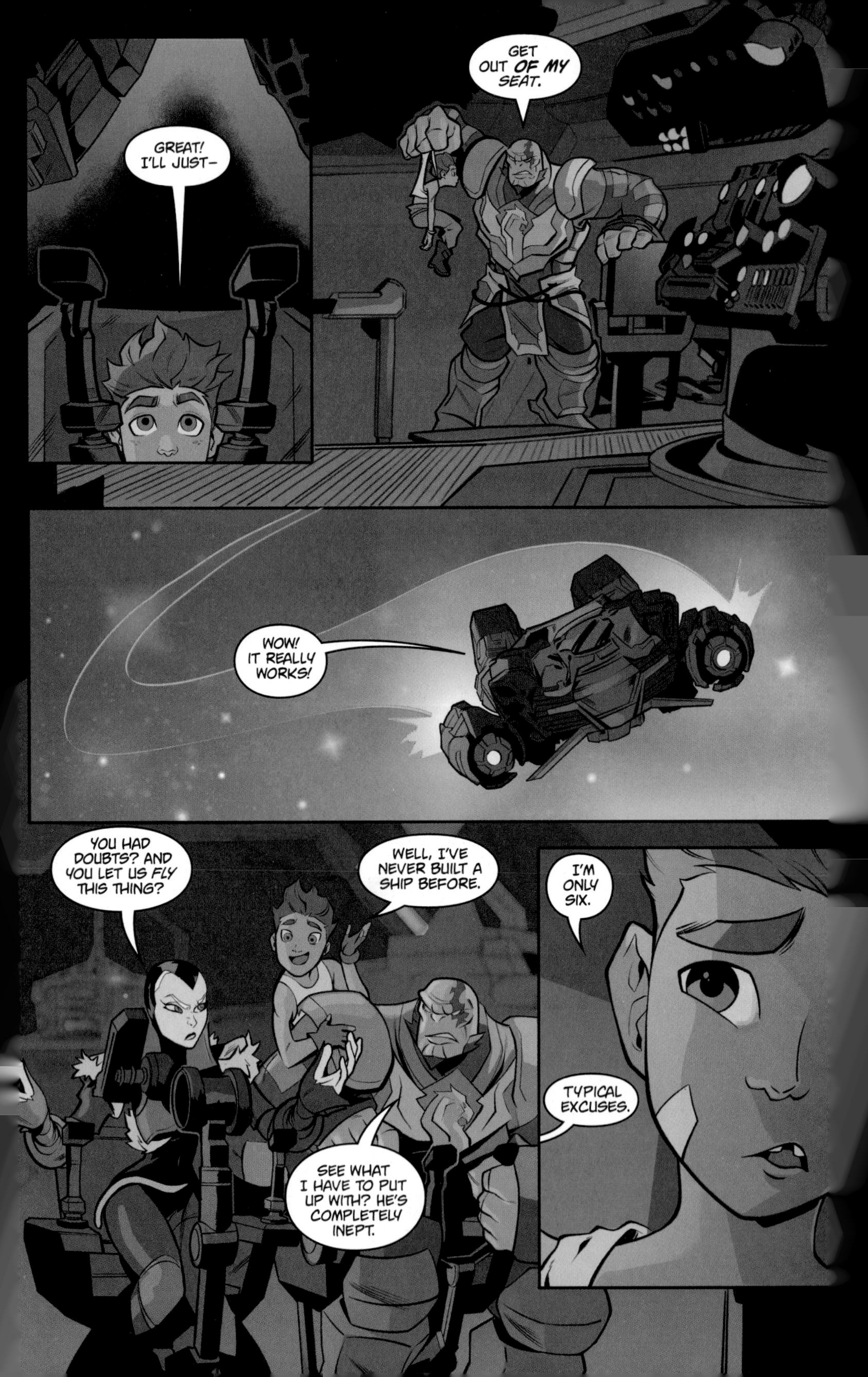
GREAT! I'LL JUST–
GET OUT OF MY SEAT.
WOW! IT REALLY WORKS!
YOU HAD DOUBTS? AND YOU LET US FLY THIS THING?
WELL, I'VE NEVER BUILT A SHIP BEFORE.
SEE WHAT I HAVE TO PUT UP WITH? HE'S COMPLETELY INEPT.
I'M ONLY SIX.
TYPICAL EXCUSES.

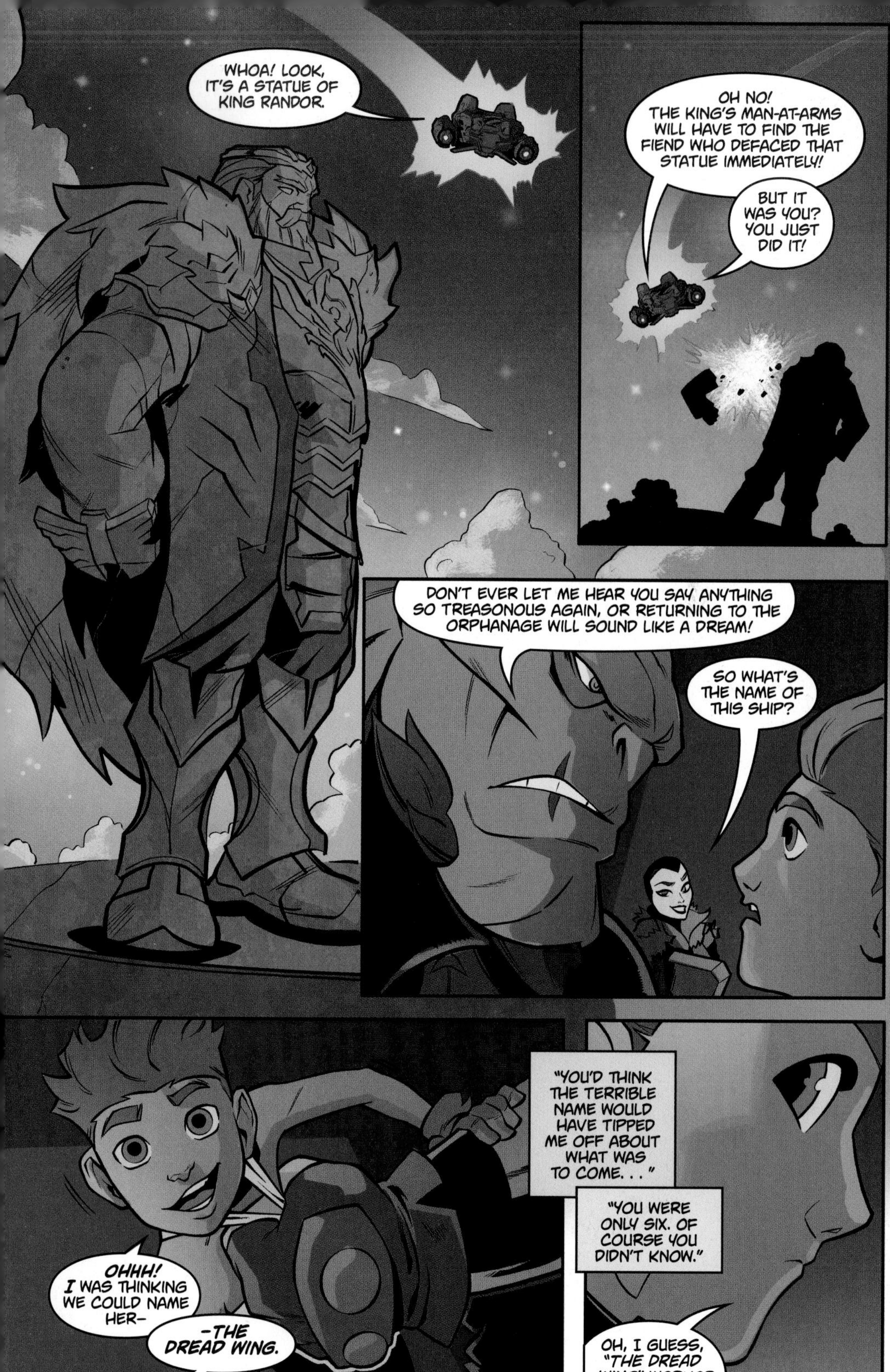
WHOA! LOOK, IT'S A STATUE OF KING RANDOR.
OH NO! THE KING'S MAN-AT-ARMS WILL HAVE TO FIND THE FIEND WHO DEFACED THAT STATUE IMMEDIATELY!
BUT IT WAS YOU? YOU JUST DID IT!
DON'T EVER LET ME HEAR YOU SAY ANYTHING SO TREASONOUS AGAIN, OR RETURNING TO THE ORPHANAGE WILL SOUND LIKE A DREAM!
SO WHAT'S THE NAME OF THIS SHIP?
OHHH! I WAS THINKING WE COULD NAME HER-
-THE DREAD WING.
"YOU'D THINK THE TERRIBLE NAME WOULD HAVE TIPPED ME OFF ABOUT WHAT WAS TO COME. . ."
"YOU WERE ONLY SIX. OF COURSE YOU DIDN'T KNOW."
OH, I GUESS, "THE DREAD WING" WORKS?

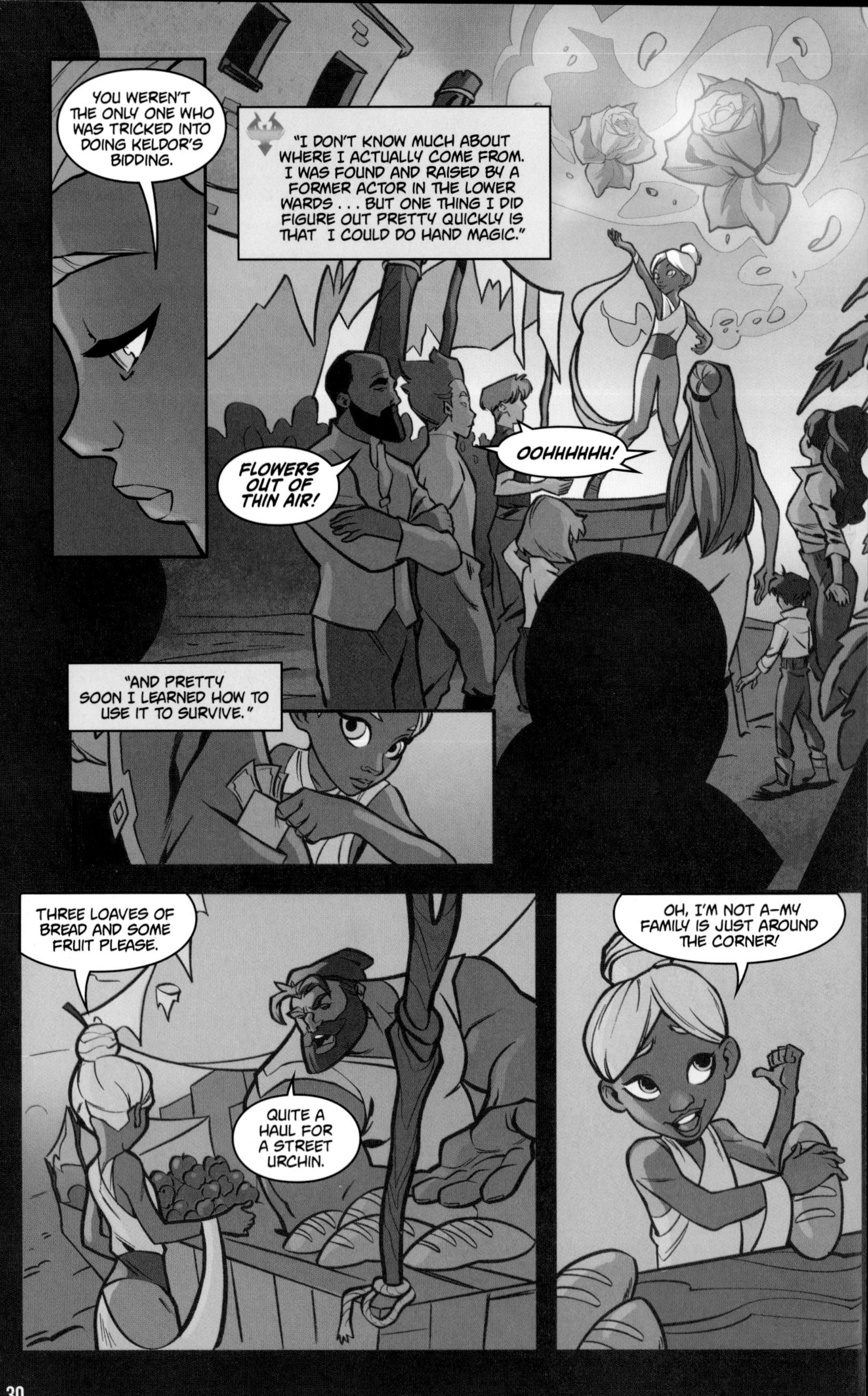

YOU WEREN'T THE ONLY ONE WHO WAS TRICKED INTO DOING KELDOR'S BIDDING.
"I DON'T KNOW MUCH ABOUT WHERE I ACTUALLY COME FROM. I WAS FOUND AND RAISED BY A FORMER ACTOR IN THE LOWER WARDS . . . BUT ONE THING I DID FIGURE OUT PRETTY QUICKLY IS THAT I COULD DO HAND MAGIC."
FLOWERS OUT OF THIN AIR!
OOHHHHHH!
"AND PRETTY SOON I LEARNED HOW TO USE IT TO SURVIVE."
THREE LOAVES OF BREAD AND SOME FRUIT PLEASE.
QUITE A HAUL FOR A STREET URCHIN.
OH, I'M NOT A—MY FAMILY IS JUST AROUND THE CORNER!

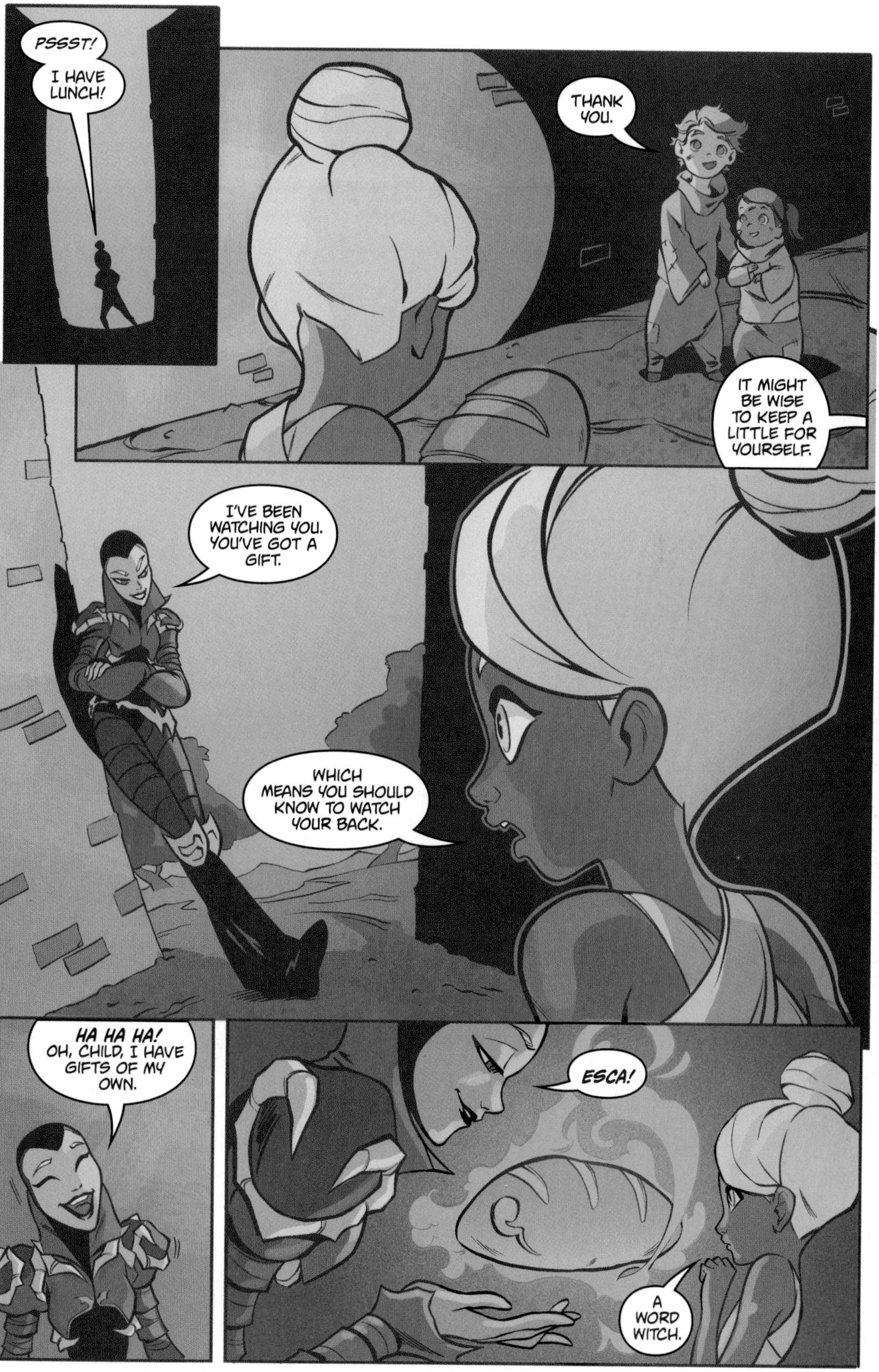
PSSST!
I HAVE LUNCH!
THANK YOU.
IT MIGHT BE WISE TO KEEP A LITTLE FOR YOURSELF.
I'VE BEEN WATCHING YOU. YOU'VE GOT A GIFT.
WHICH MEANS YOU SHOULD KNOW TO WATCH YOUR BACK.
HA HA HA! OH, CHILD, I HAVE GIFTS OF MY OWN.
ESCA!
A WORD WITCH.

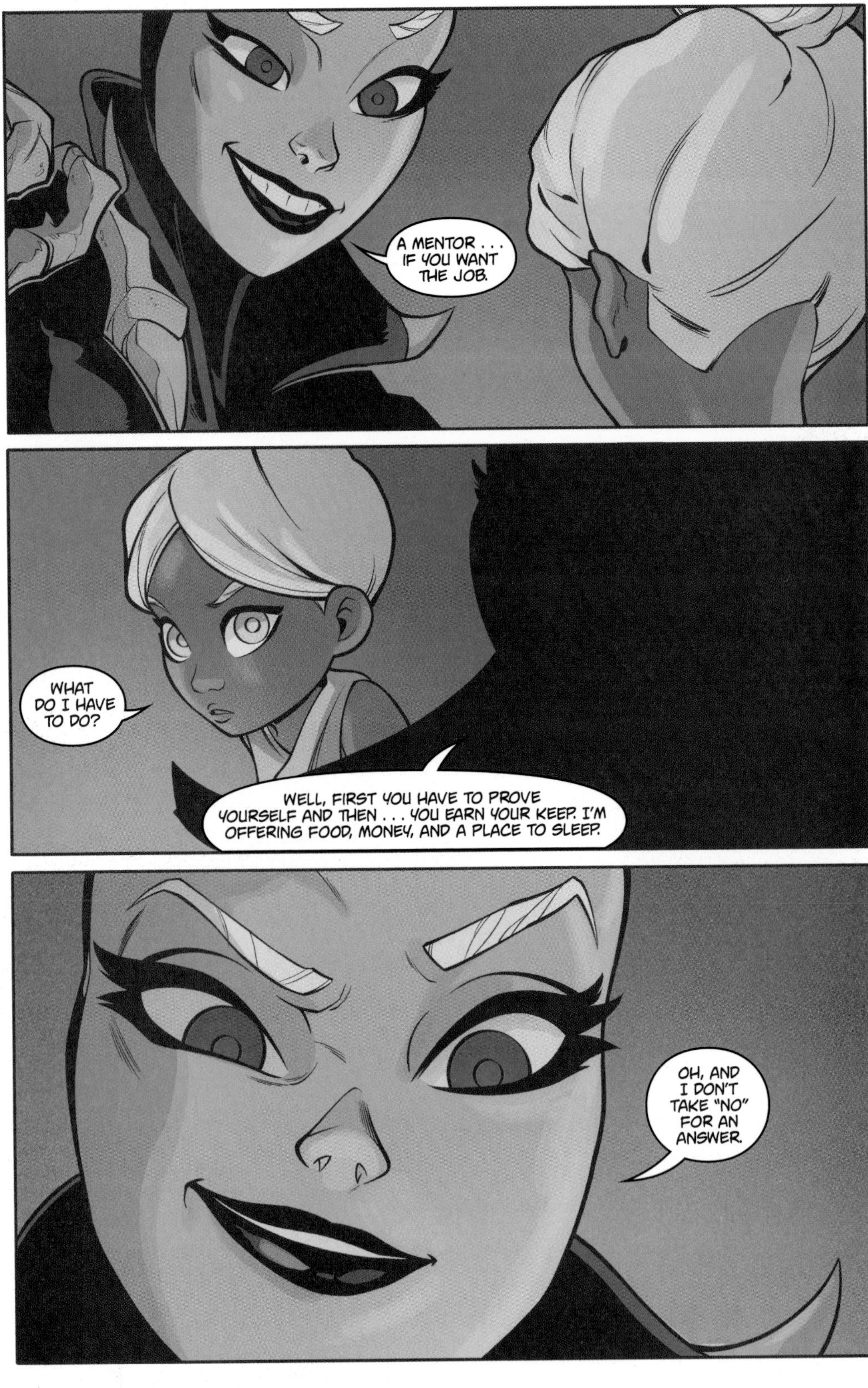
A MENTOR . . . IF YOU WANT THE JOB.
WHAT DO I HAVE TO DO?
WELL, FIRST YOU HAVE TO PROVE YOURSELF AND THEN . . . YOU EARN YOUR KEEP. I'M OFFERING FOOD, MONEY, AND A PLACE TO SLEEP.
OH, AND I DON'T TAKE "NO" FOR AN ANSWER.

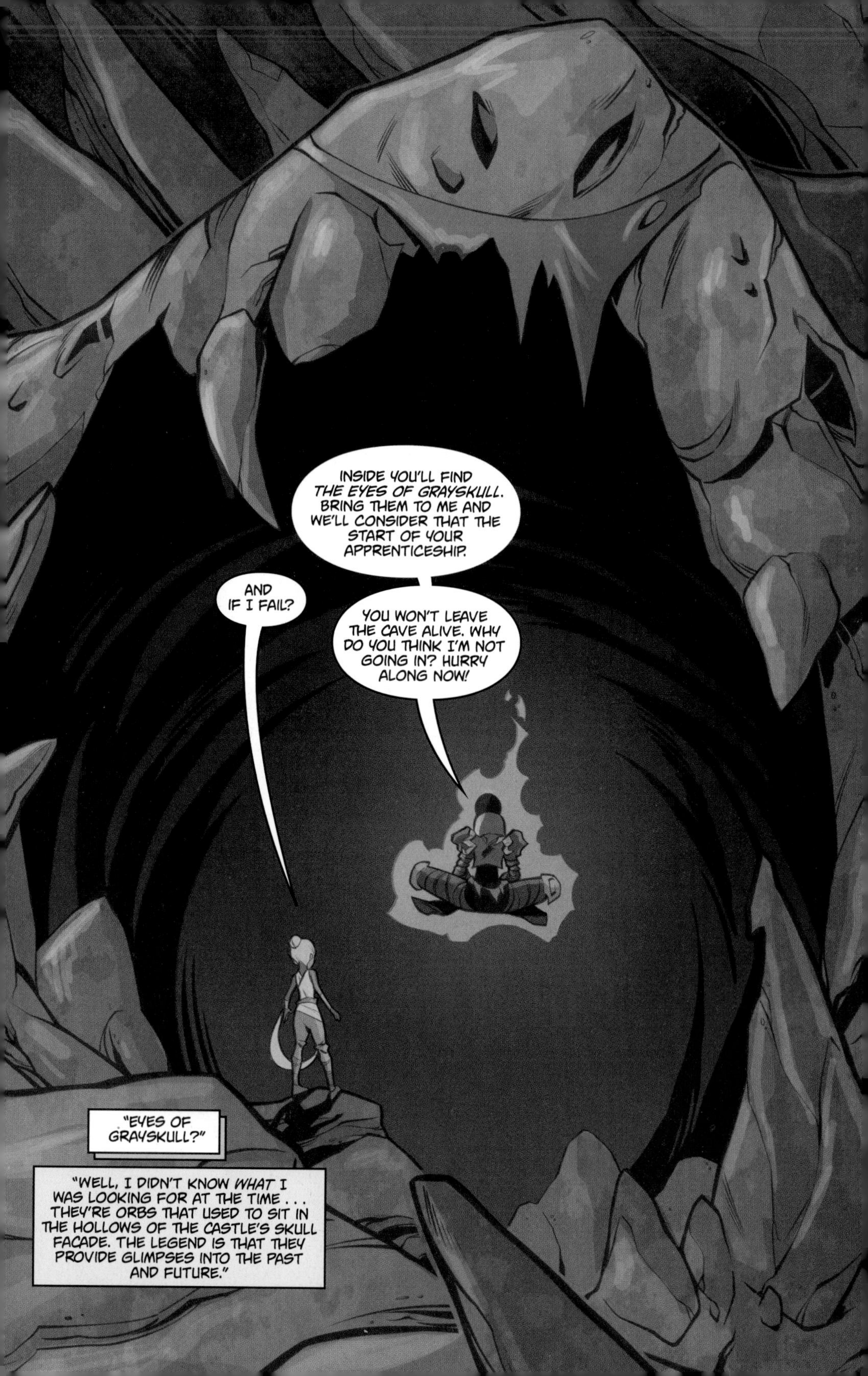
INSIDE YOU'LL FIND *THE EYES OF GRAYSKULL*. BRING THEM TO ME AND WE'LL CONSIDER THAT THE START OF YOUR APPRENTICESHIP.
AND IF I FAIL?
YOU WON'T LEAVE THE CAVE ALIVE. WHY DO YOU THINK I'M NOT GOING IN? HURRY ALONG NOW!
"EYES OF GRAYSKULL?"
"WELL, I DIDN'T KNOW *WHAT* I WAS LOOKING FOR AT THE TIME . . . THEY'RE ORBS THAT USED TO SIT IN THE HOLLOWS OF THE CASTLE'S SKULL FACADE. THE LEGEND IS THAT THEY PROVIDE GLIMPSES INTO THE PAST AND FUTURE."

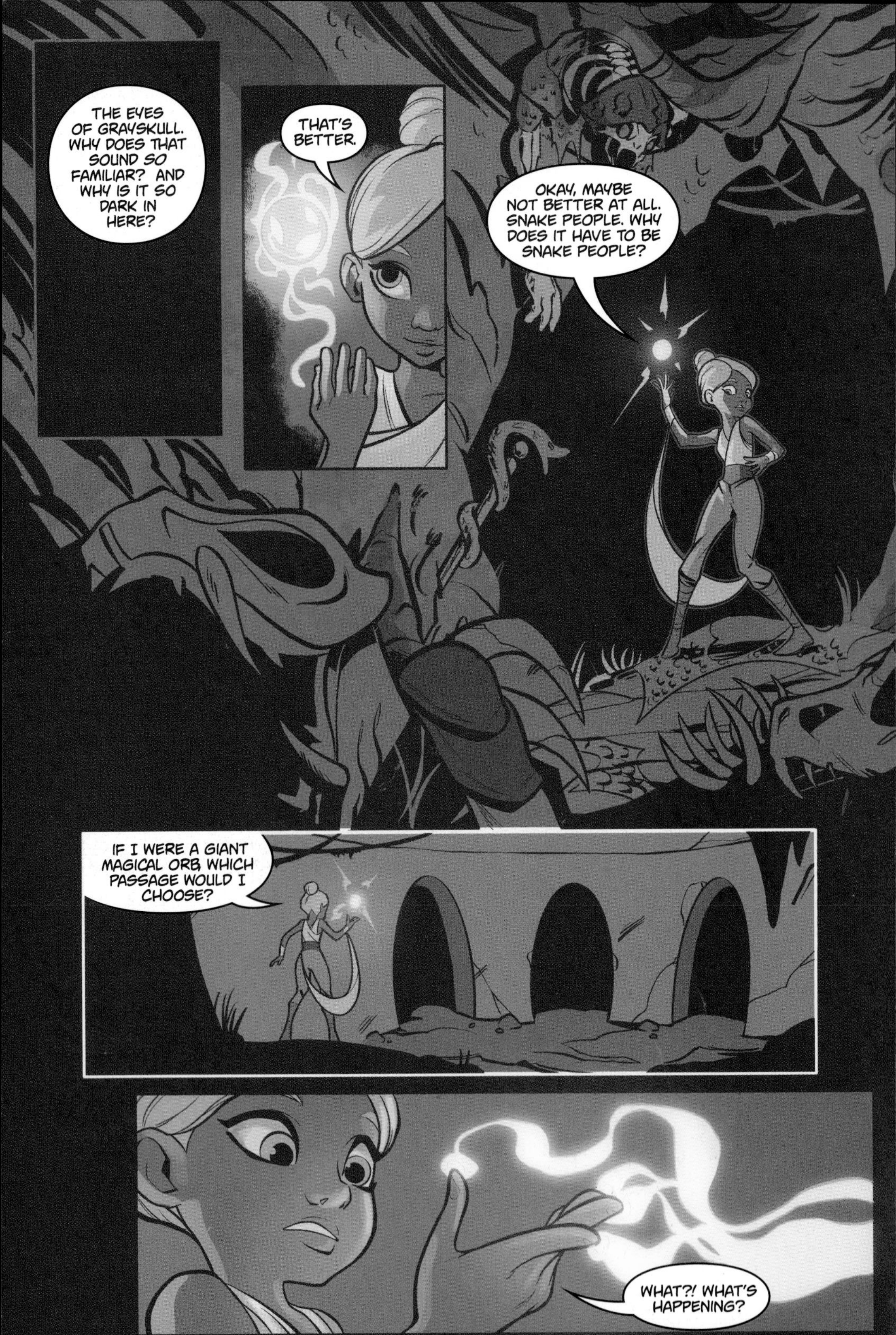
THE EYES OF GRAYSKULL. WHY DOES THAT SOUND SO FAMILIAR? AND WHY IS IT SO DARK IN HERE?
THAT'S BETTER.
OKAY, MAYBE NOT BETTER AT ALL. SNAKE PEOPLE. WHY DOES IT HAVE TO BE SNAKE PEOPLE?
IF I WERE A GIANT MAGICAL ORB, WHICH PASSAGE WOULD I CHOOSE?
WHAT?! WHAT'S HAPPENING?

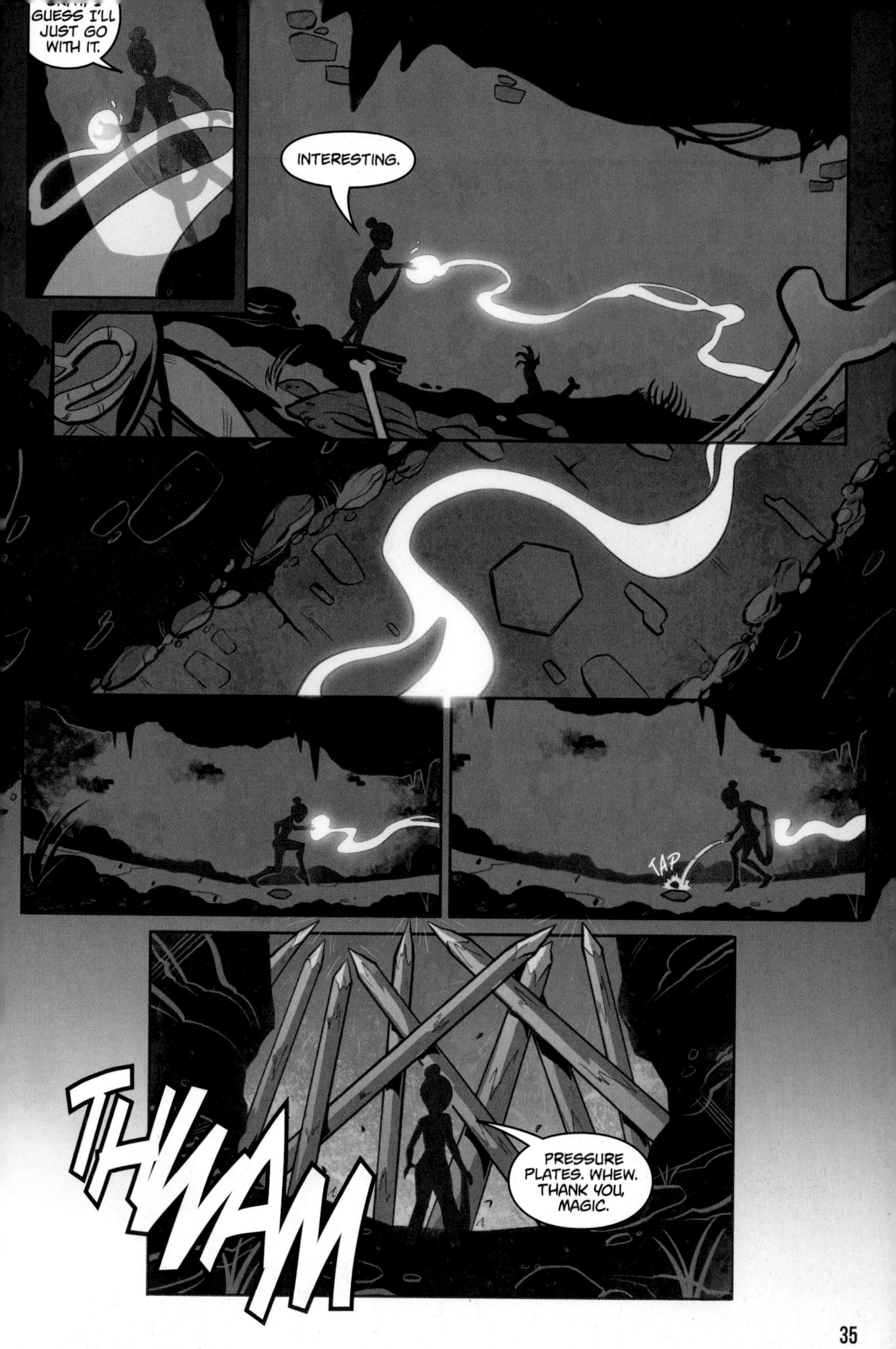
GUESS I'LL JUST GO WITH IT.
INTERESTING.
TAP
THWAM
PRESSURE PLATES. WHEW. THANK YOU, MAGIC.

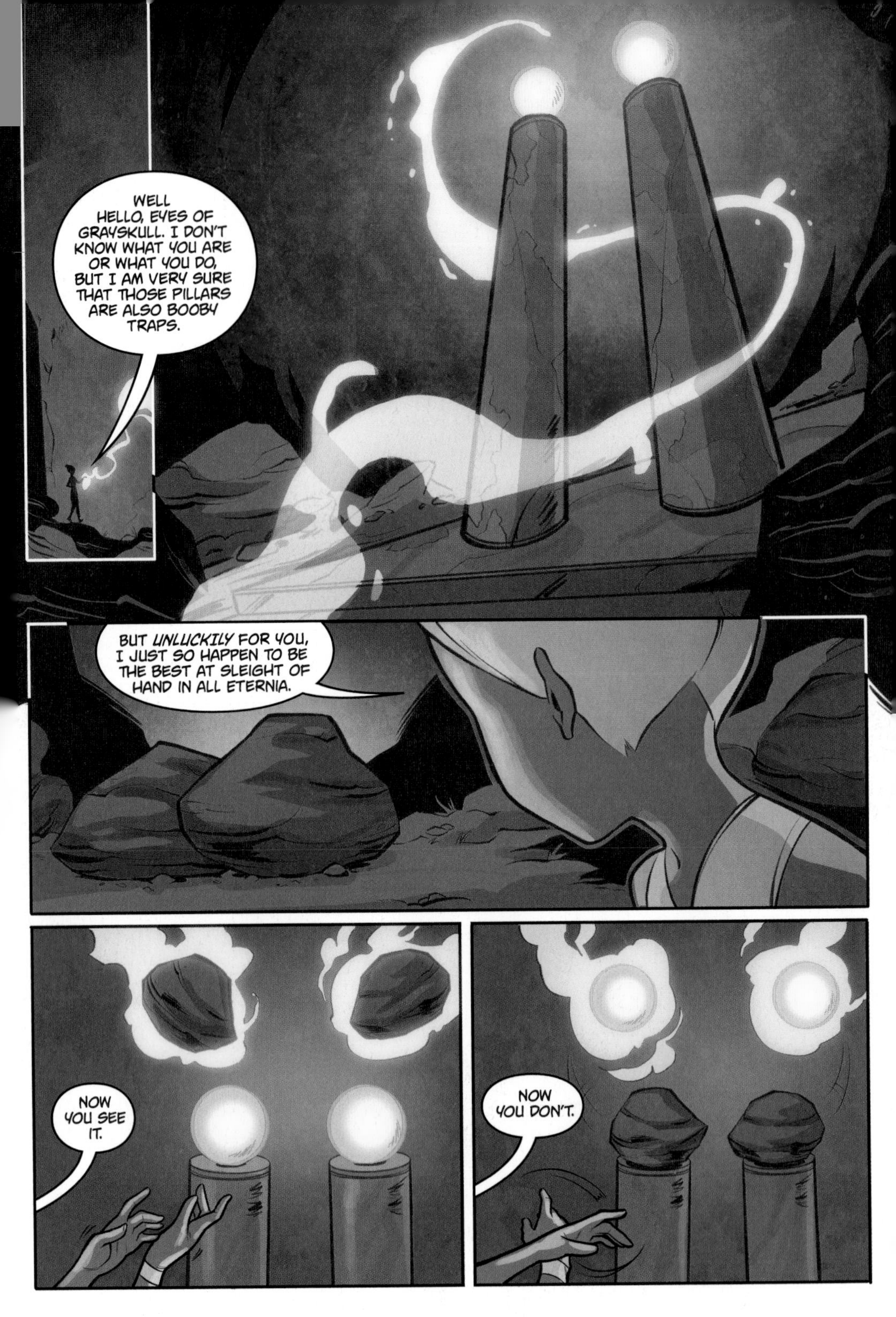
WELL HELLO, EYES OF GRAYSKULL. I DON'T KNOW WHAT YOU ARE OR WHAT YOU DO, BUT I AM VERY SURE THAT THOSE PILLARS ARE ALSO BOOBY TRAPS.
BUT *UNLUCKILY* FOR YOU, I JUST SO HAPPEN TO BE THE BEST AT SLEIGHT OF HAND IN ALL ETERNIA.
NOW YOU SEE IT.
NOW YOU DON'T.

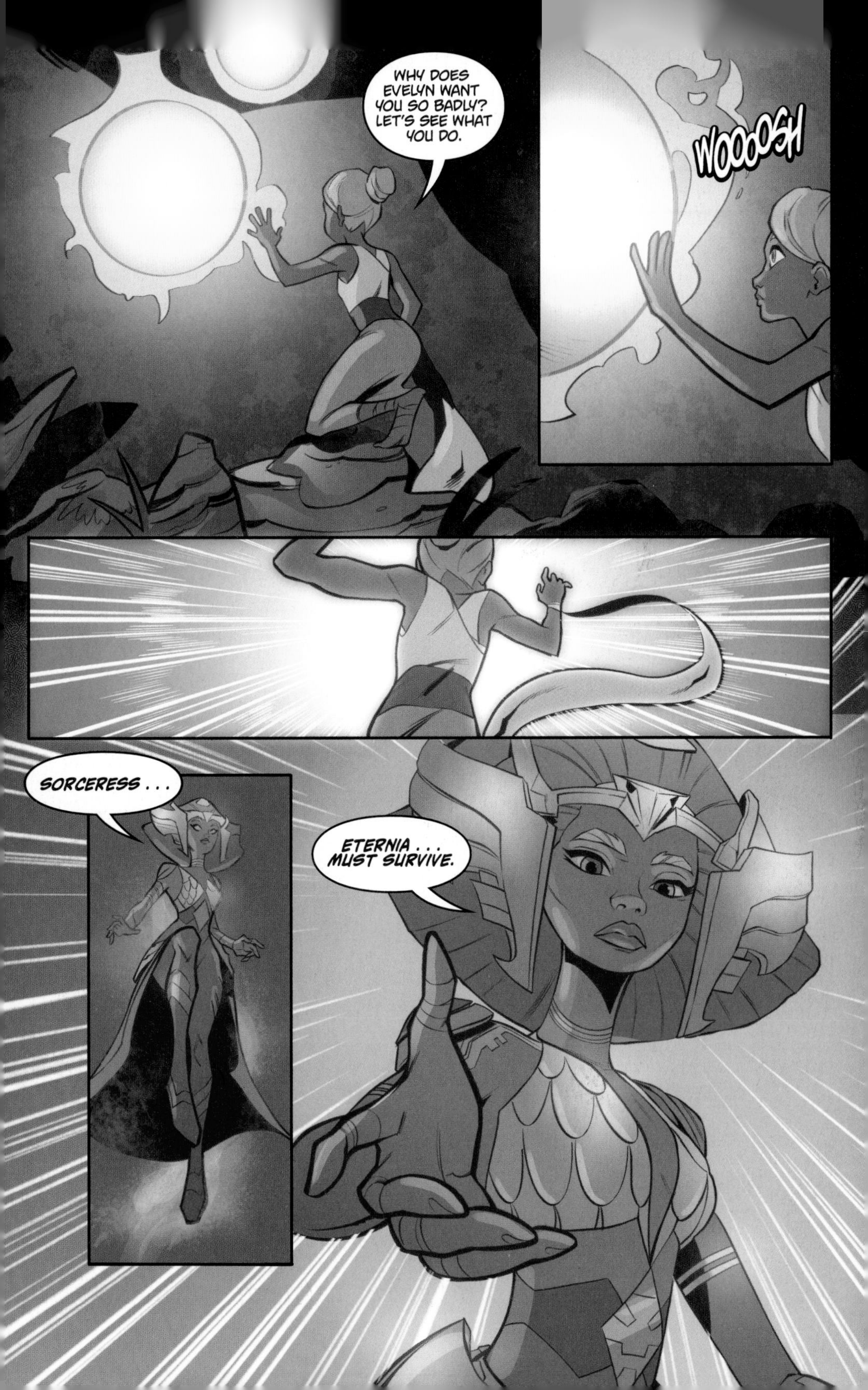
WHY DOES EVELYN WANT YOU SO BADLY? LET'S SEE WHAT YOU DO.
WOOOOSH
SORCERESS . . .
ETERNIA . . . MUST SURVIVE.

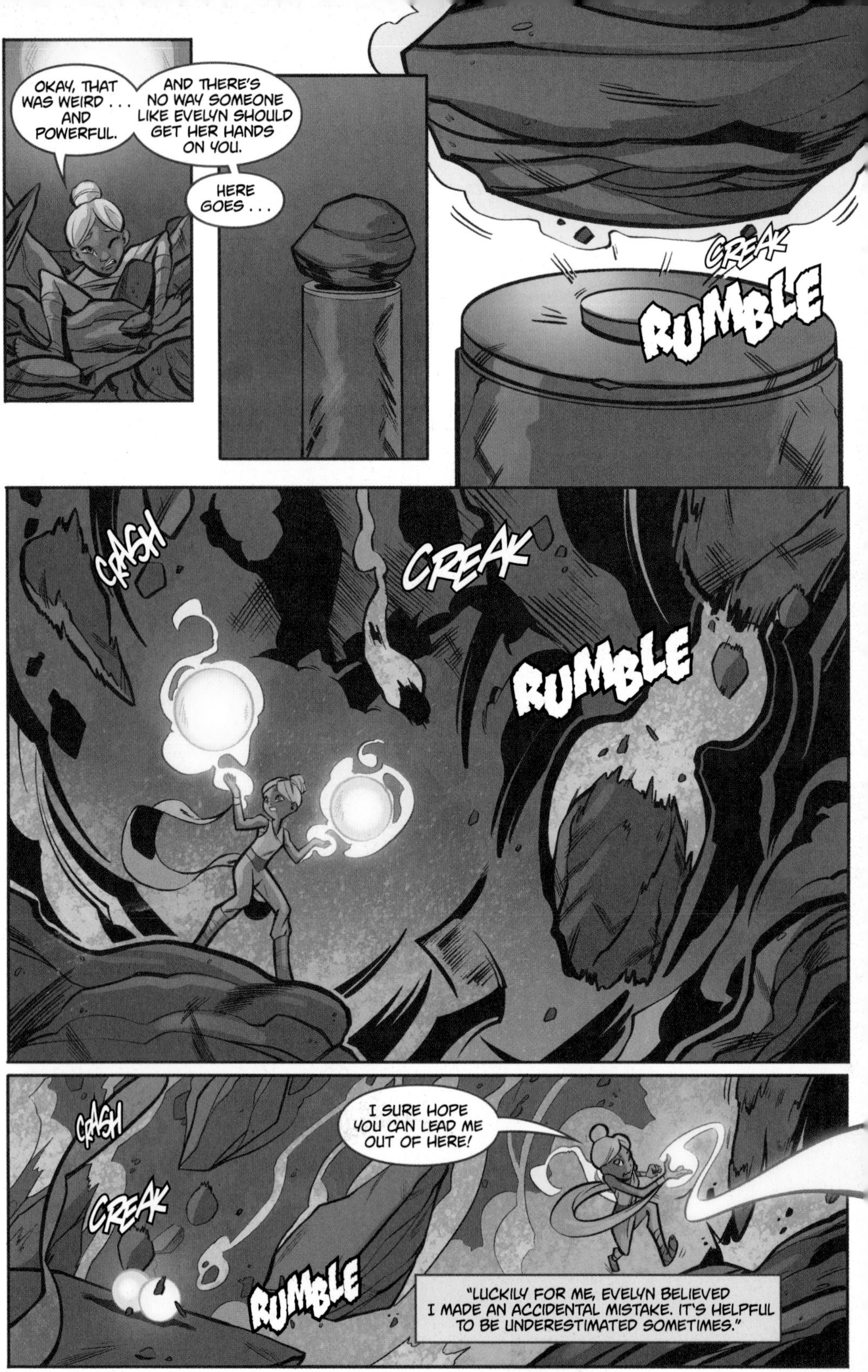
OKAY, THAT WAS WEIRD . . . AND POWERFUL.
AND THERE'S NO WAY SOMEONE LIKE EVELYN SHOULD GET HER HANDS ON YOU.
HERE GOES . . .
CREAK
RUMBLE
CRASH
CREAK
RUMBLE
CRASH
CREAK
RUMBLE
I SURE HOPE YOU CAN LEAD ME OUT OF HERE!
"LUCKILY FOR ME, EVELYN BELIEVED I MADE AN ACCIDENTAL MISTAKE. IT'S HELPFUL TO BE UNDERESTIMATED SOMETIMES."

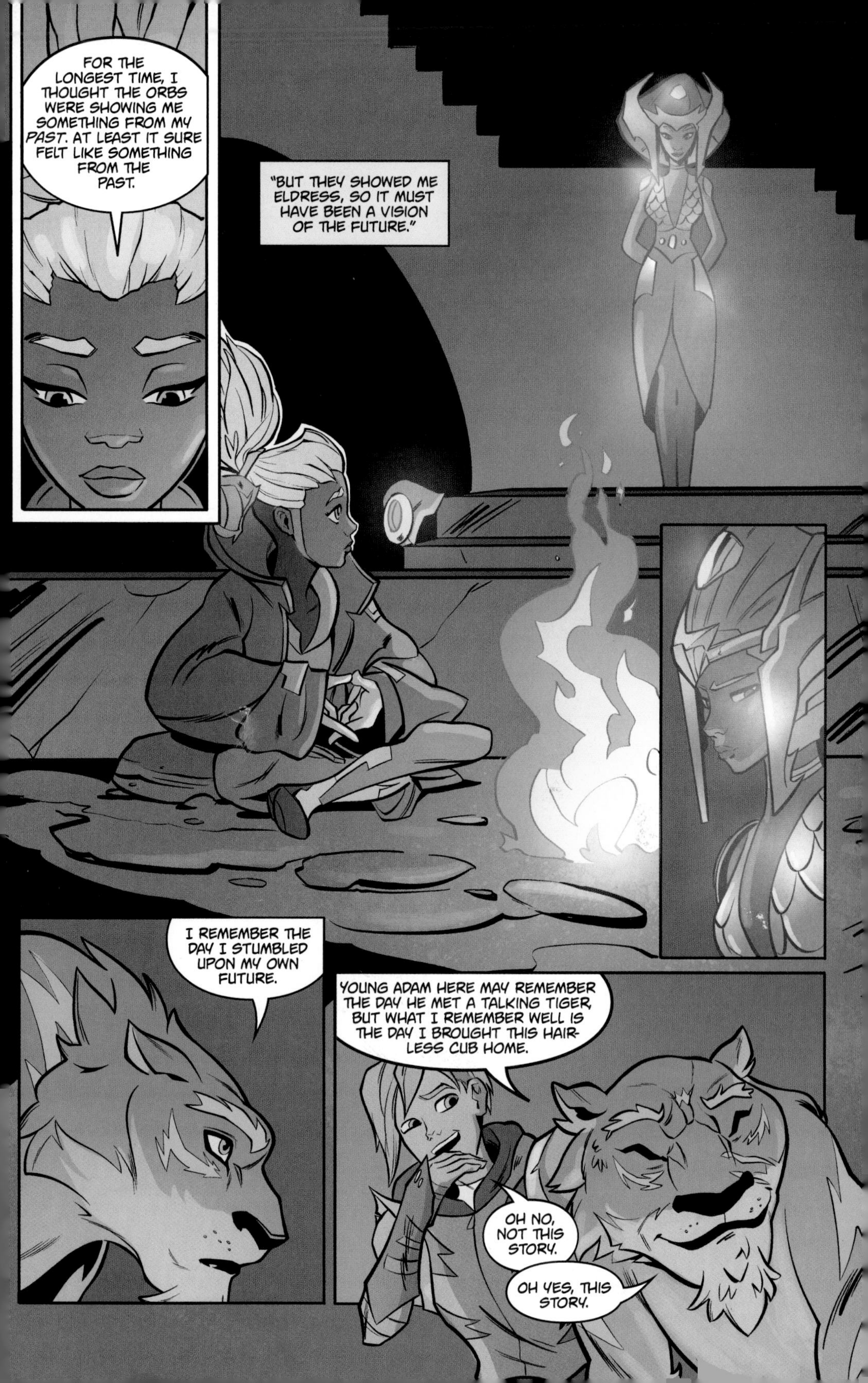
FOR THE LONGEST TIME, I THOUGHT THE ORBS WERE SHOWING ME SOMETHING FROM MY *PAST*. AT LEAST IT SURE FELT LIKE SOMETHING FROM THE PAST.
"BUT THEY SHOWED ME ELDRESS, SO IT MUST HAVE BEEN A VISION OF THE FUTURE."
I REMEMBER THE DAY I STUMBLED UPON MY OWN FUTURE.
YOUNG ADAM HERE MAY REMEMBER THE DAY HE MET A TALKING TIGER, BUT WHAT I REMEMBER WELL IS THE DAY I BROUGHT THIS HAIR-LESS CUB HOME.
OH NO, NOT THIS STORY.
OH YES, THIS STORY.

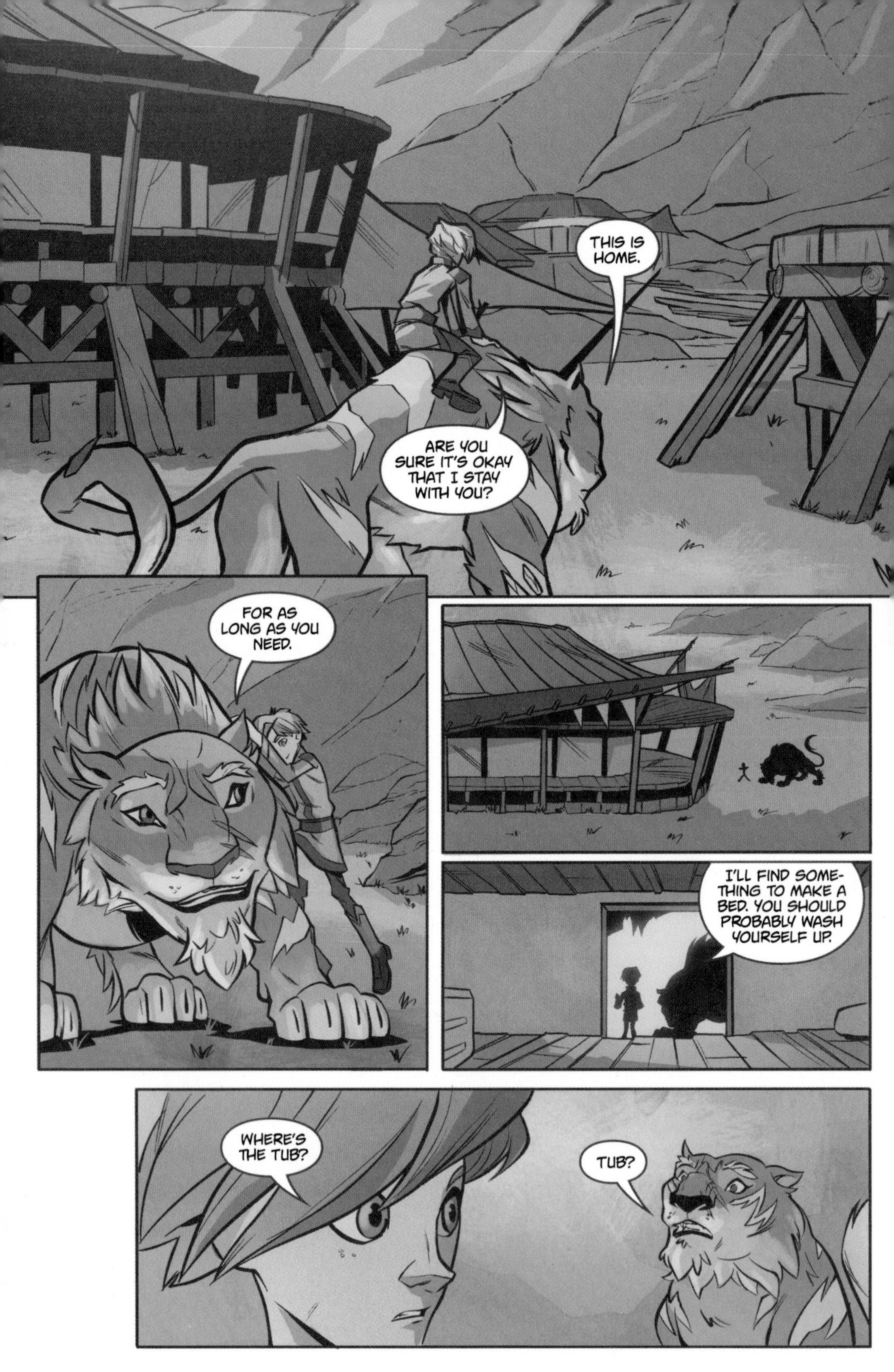

THIS IS HOME.
ARE YOU SURE IT'S OKAY THAT I STAY WITH YOU?
FOR AS LONG AS YOU NEED.
I'LL FIND SOME-THING TO MAKE A BED. YOU SHOULD PROBABLY WASH YOURSELF UP.
WHERE'S THE TUB?
TUB?

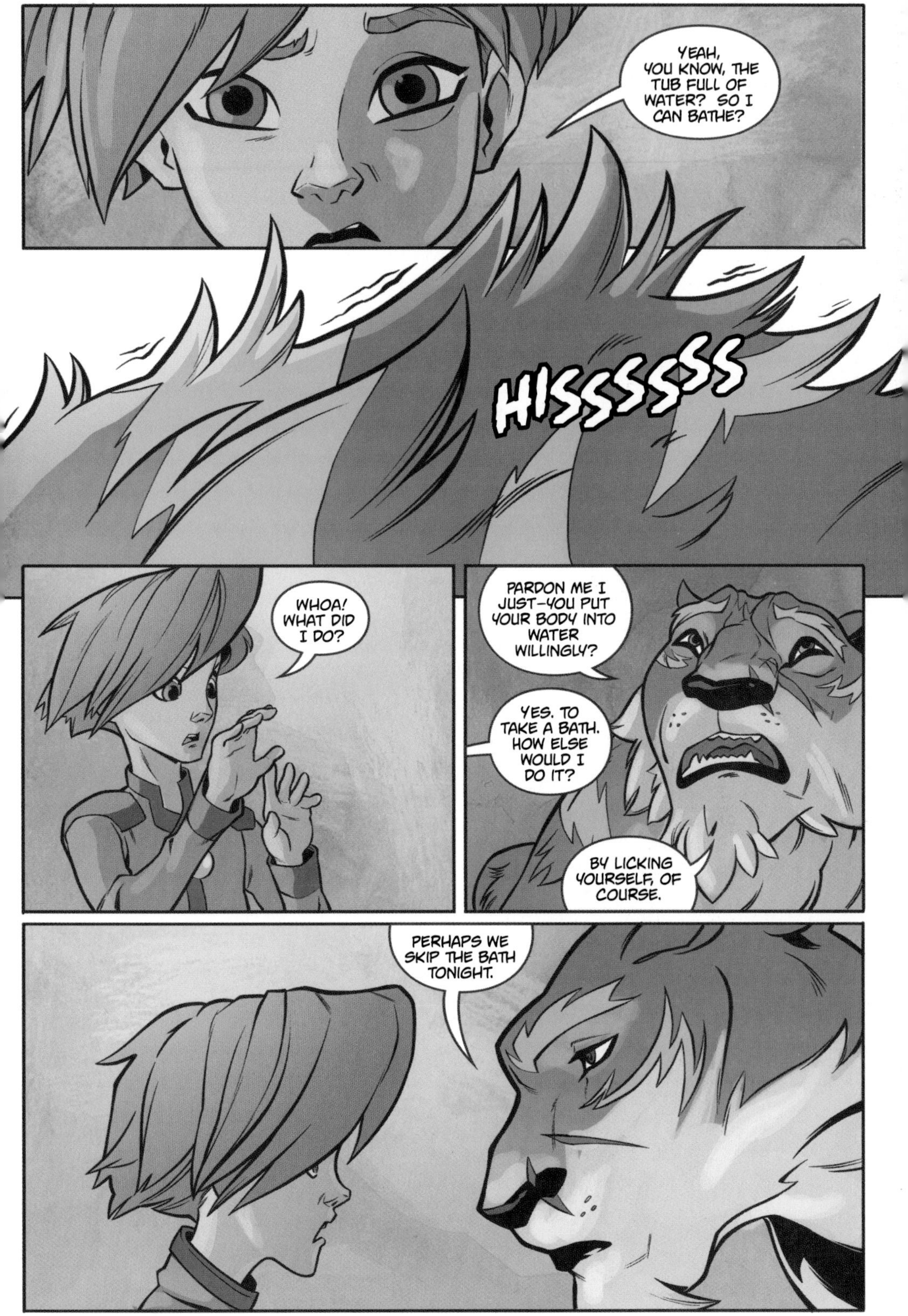
YEAH, YOU KNOW, THE TUB FULL OF WATER? SO I CAN BATHE?
HISSSSSS
WHOA! WHAT DID I DO?
PARDON ME I JUST—YOU PUT YOUR BODY INTO WATER WILLINGLY?
YES. TO TAKE A BATH. HOW ELSE WOULD I DO IT?
BY LICKING YOURSELF, OF COURSE.
PERHAPS WE SKIP THE BATH TONIGHT.

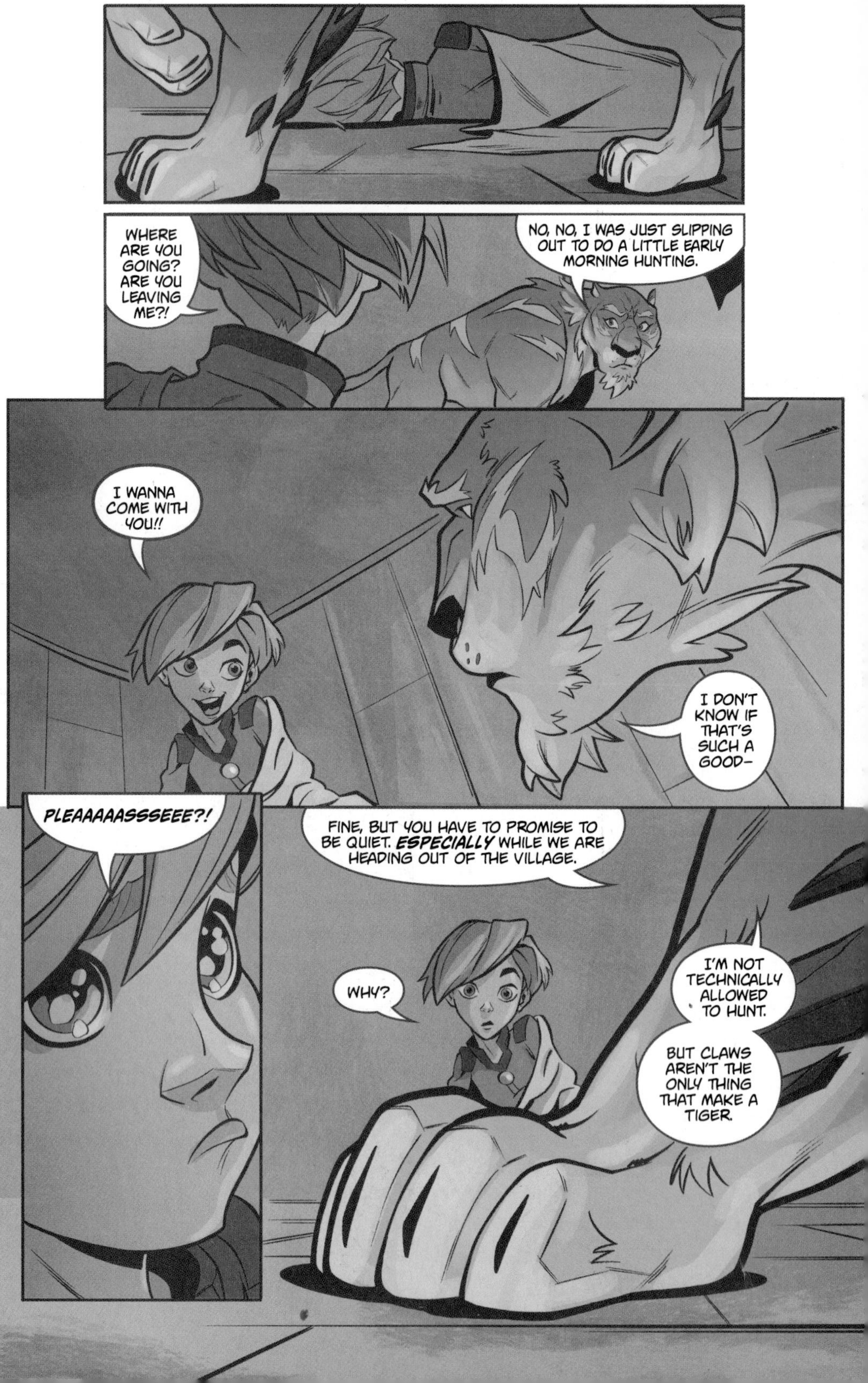
WHERE ARE YOU GOING? ARE YOU LEAVING ME?!
NO, NO, I WAS JUST SLIPPING OUT TO DO A LITTLE EARLY MORNING HUNTING.
I WANNA COME WITH YOU!!
I DON'T KNOW IF THAT'S SUCH A GOOD–
PLEAAAAASSSEEE?!
FINE, BUT YOU HAVE TO PROMISE TO BE QUIET. *ESPECIALLY* WHILE WE ARE HEADING OUT OF THE VILLAGE.
WHY?
I'M NOT TECHNICALLY ALLOWED TO HUNT.
BUT CLAWS AREN'T THE ONLY THING THAT MAKE A TIGER.

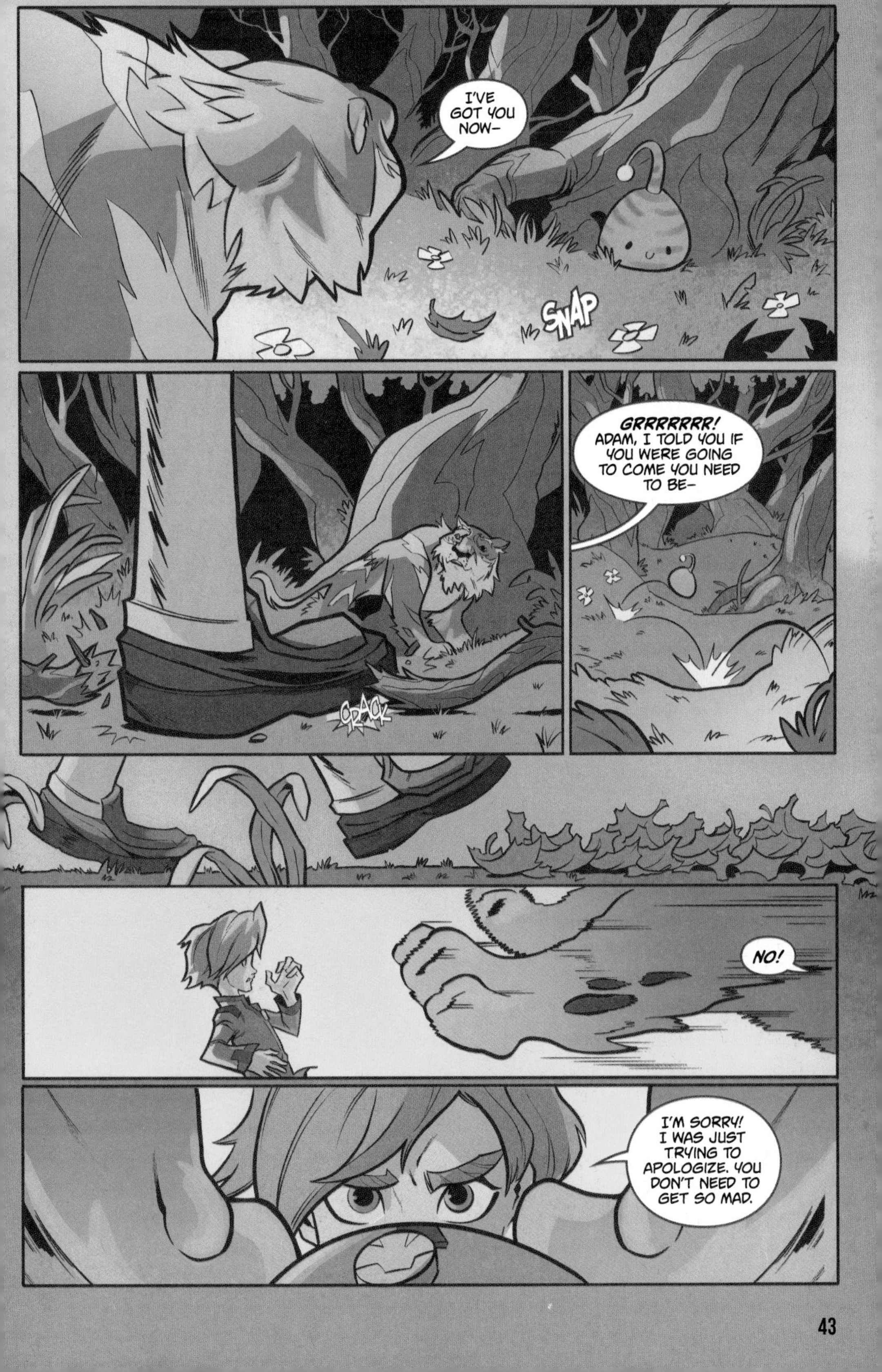
I'VE GOT YOU NOW-
SNAP
CRACK
GRRRRRRR! ADAM, I TOLD YOU IF YOU WERE GOING TO COME YOU NEED TO BE-
NO!
I'M SORRY! I WAS JUST TRYING TO APOLOGIZE. YOU DON'T NEED TO GET SO MAD.

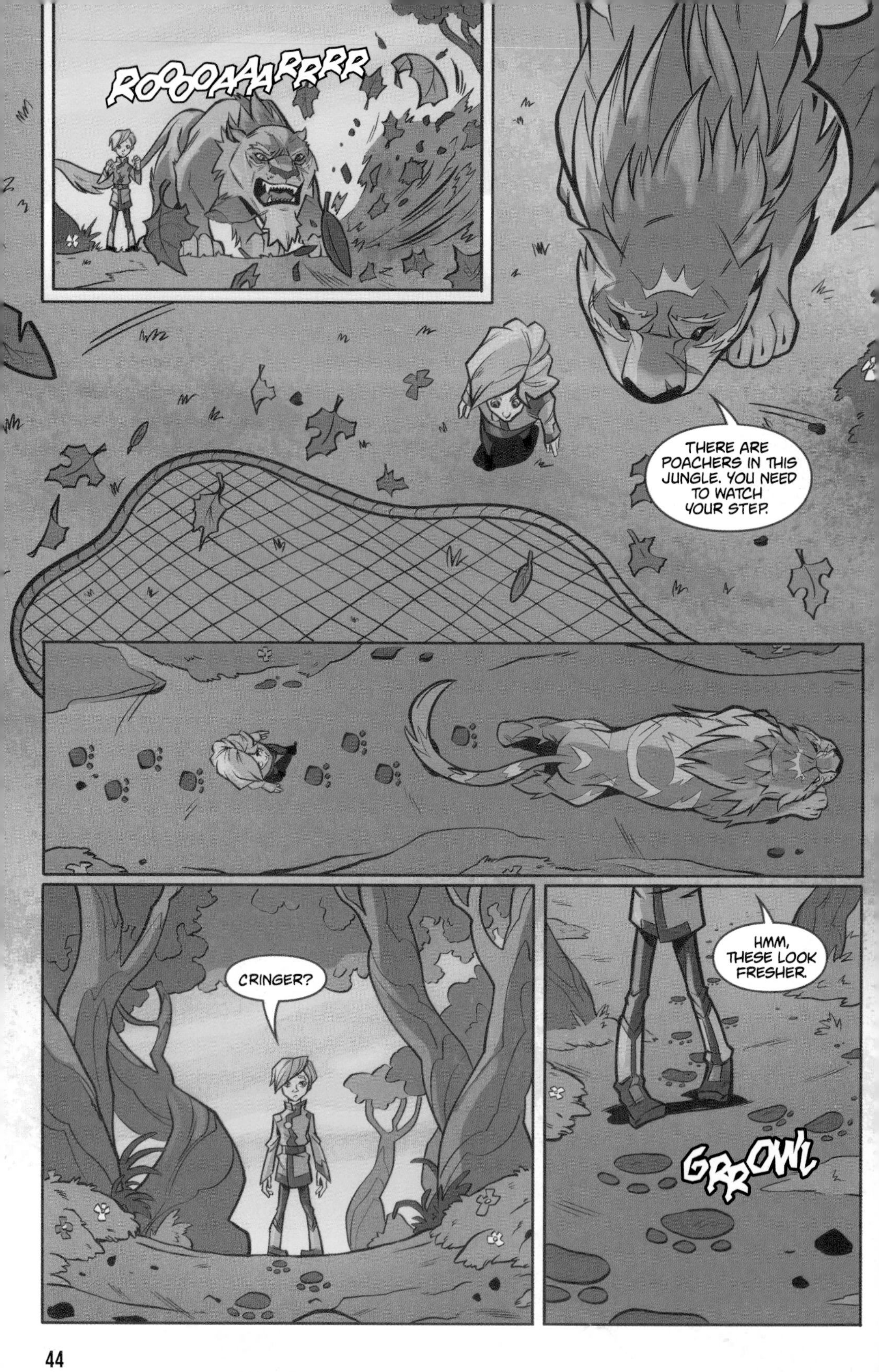
ROOOOAAARRRR
THERE ARE POACHERS IN THIS JUNGLE. YOU NEED TO WATCH YOUR STEP.
CRINGER?
HMM, THESE LOOK FRESHER.
GRROWL

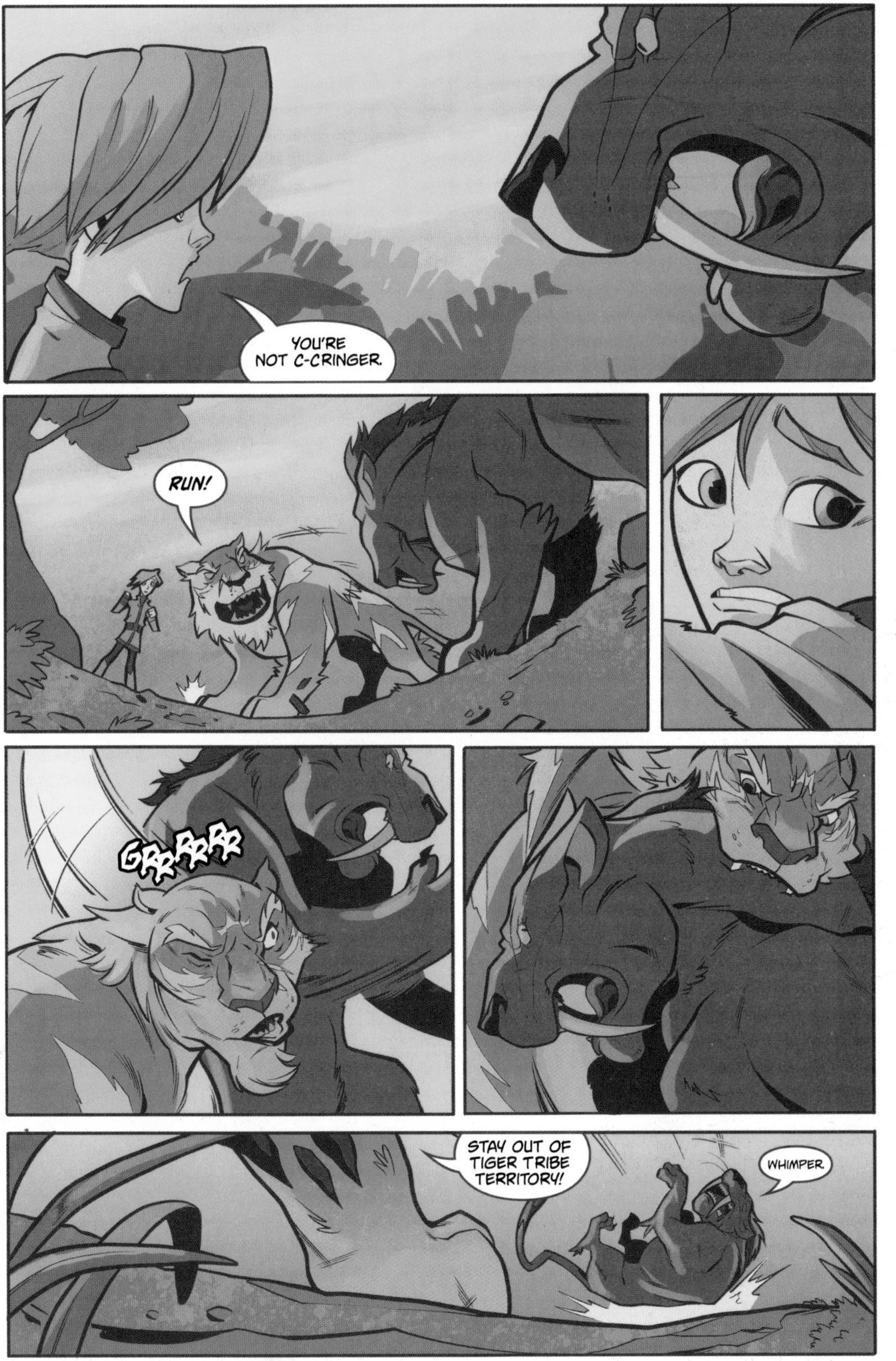
YOU'RE NOT C-CRINGER.
RUN!
GRRRRRR
STAY OUT OF TIGER TRIBE TERRITORY!
WHIMPER.

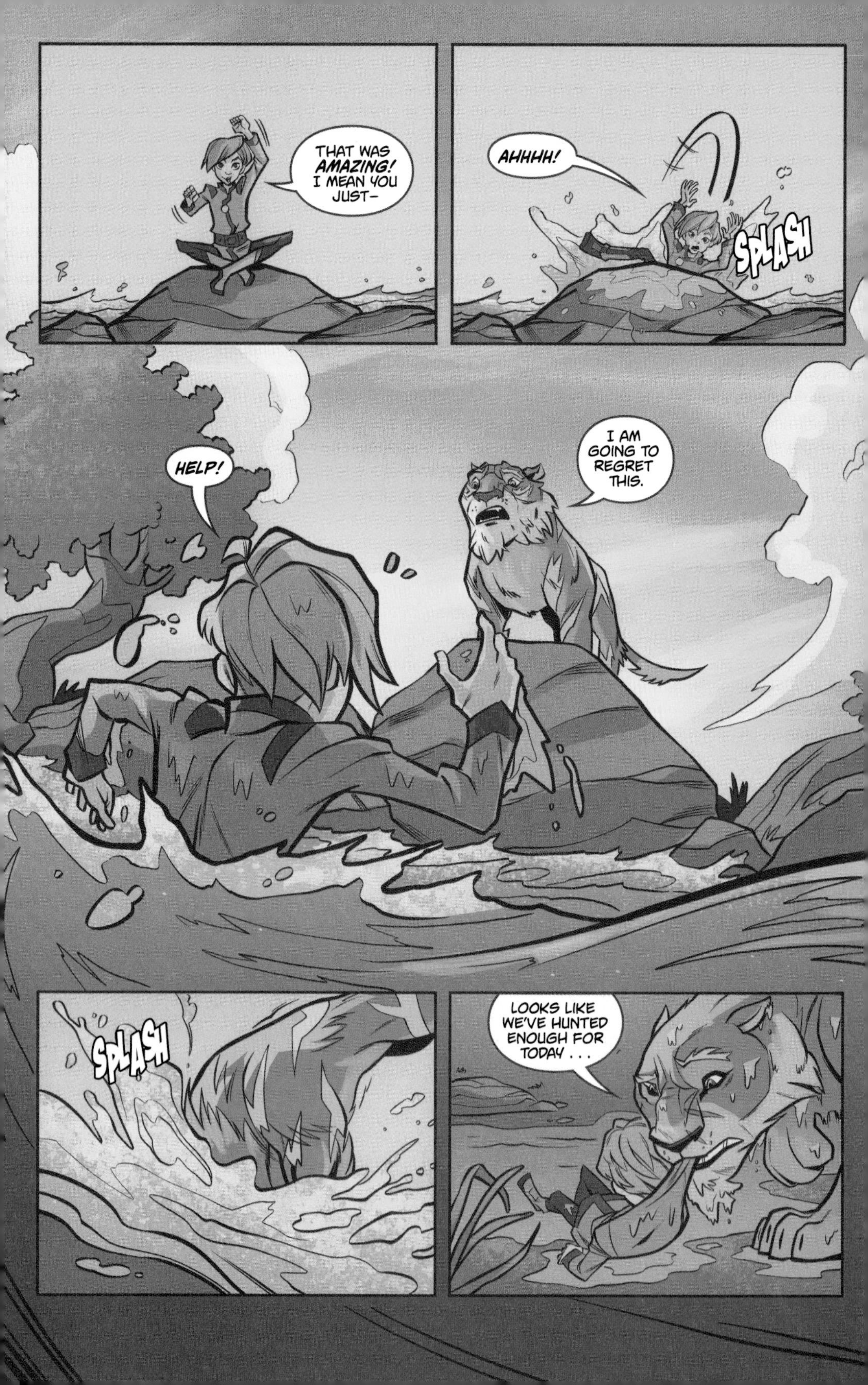
THAT WAS AMAZING! I MEAN YOU JUST–
AHHHH!
SPLASH
HELP!
I AM GOING TO REGRET THIS.
SPLASH
LOOKS LIKE WE'VE HUNTED ENOUGH FOR TODAY . . .

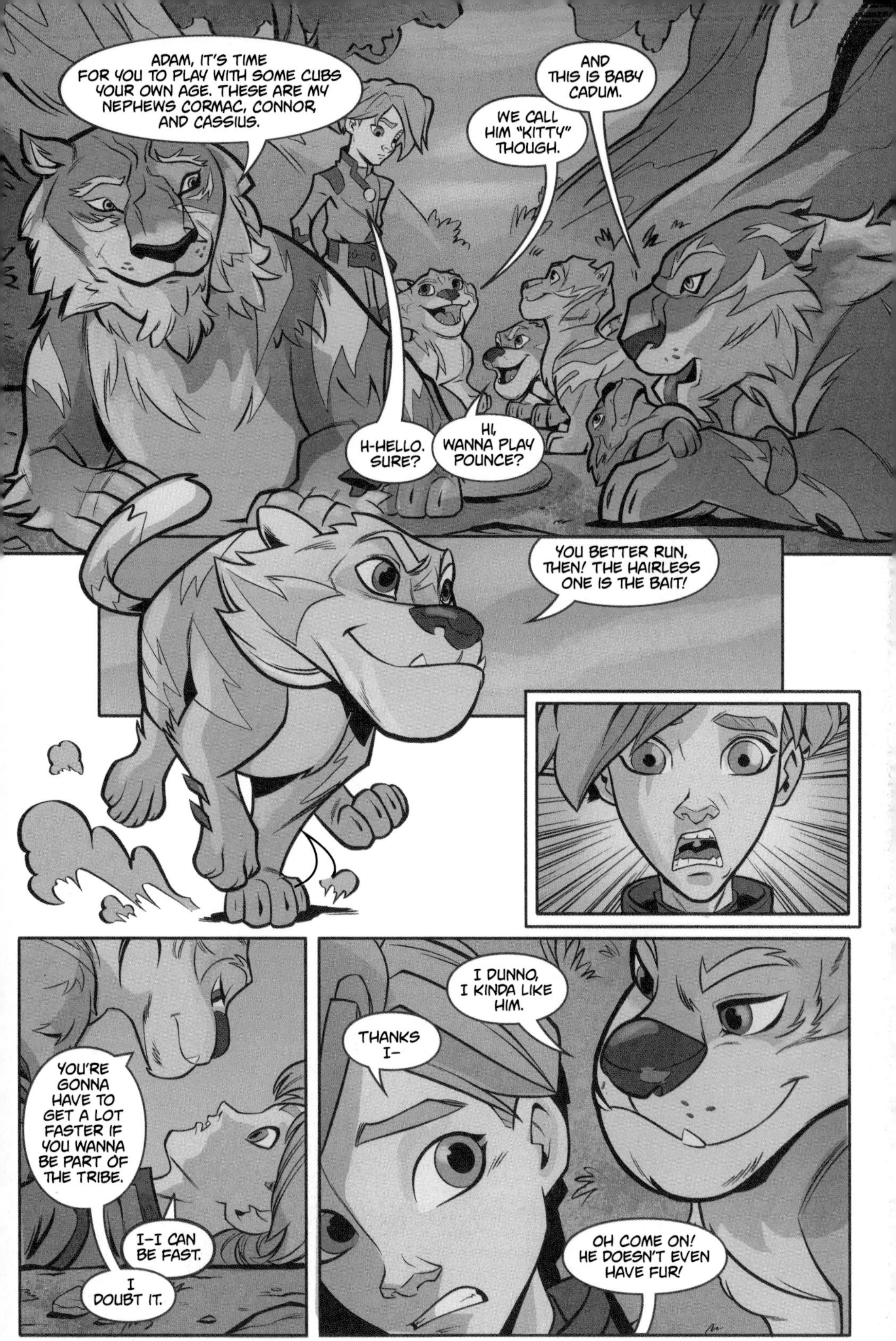
ADAM, IT'S TIME FOR YOU TO PLAY WITH SOME CUBS YOUR OWN AGE. THESE ARE MY NEPHEWS CORMAC, CONNOR, AND CASSIUS.
AND THIS IS BABY CADUM.
WE CALL HIM "KITTY" THOUGH.
H-HELLO. SURE?
HI, WANNA PLAY POUNCE?
YOU BETTER RUN, THEN! THE HAIRLESS ONE IS THE BAIT!
YOU'RE GONNA HAVE TO GET A LOT FASTER IF YOU WANNA BE PART OF THE TRIBE.
I-I CAN BE FAST.
I DOUBT IT.
I DUNNO, I KINDA LIKE HIM.
THANKS I-
OH COME ON! HE DOESN'T EVEN HAVE FUR!

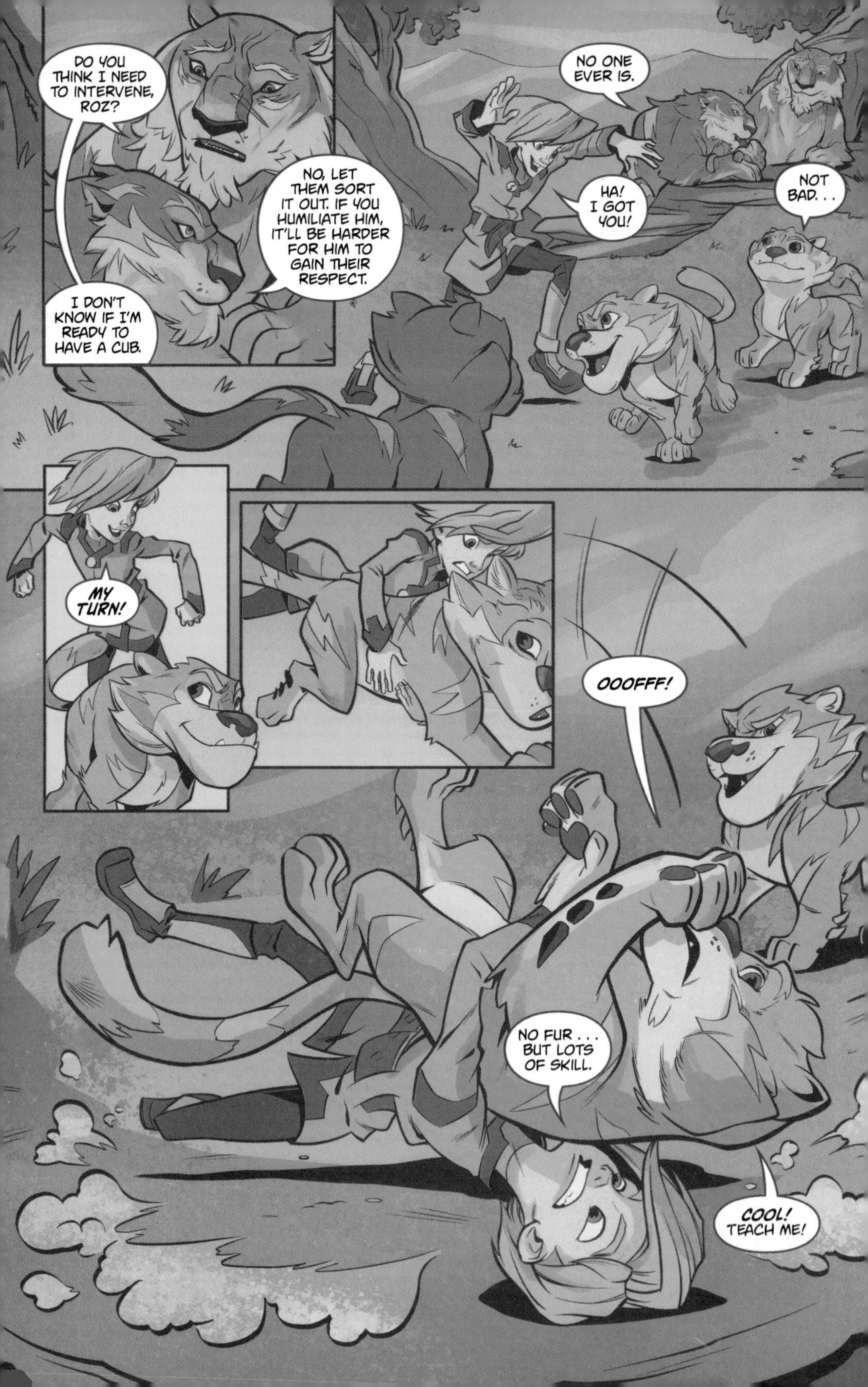
DO YOU THINK I NEED TO INTERVENE, ROZ?
NO, LET THEM SORT IT OUT. IF YOU HUMILIATE HIM, IT'LL BE HARDER FOR HIM TO GAIN THEIR RESPECT.
I DON'T KNOW IF I'M READY TO HAVE A CUB.
NO ONE EVER IS.
HA! I GOT YOU!
NOT BAD. . .
MY TURN!
OOOFFF!
NO FUR . . . BUT LOTS OF SKILL.
COOL! TEACH ME!

I'D LOVE TO!

WELL, YOU STILL SMELL FUNNY . . . AND YOU DON'T HAVE ANY CLAWS.

GRRRRR

NOT THAT THERE IS ANYTHING WRONG WITH BEING CLAW-LESS. LLOTS OF THE BEST TIGERS ARE . . JUST THE OTHER STUFF!

ABOUT THE CLAW THING . . .

I HAVE AN IDEA FOR THAT TOO.

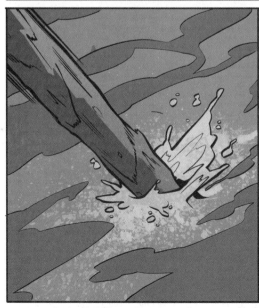

WHOA!

COOL!

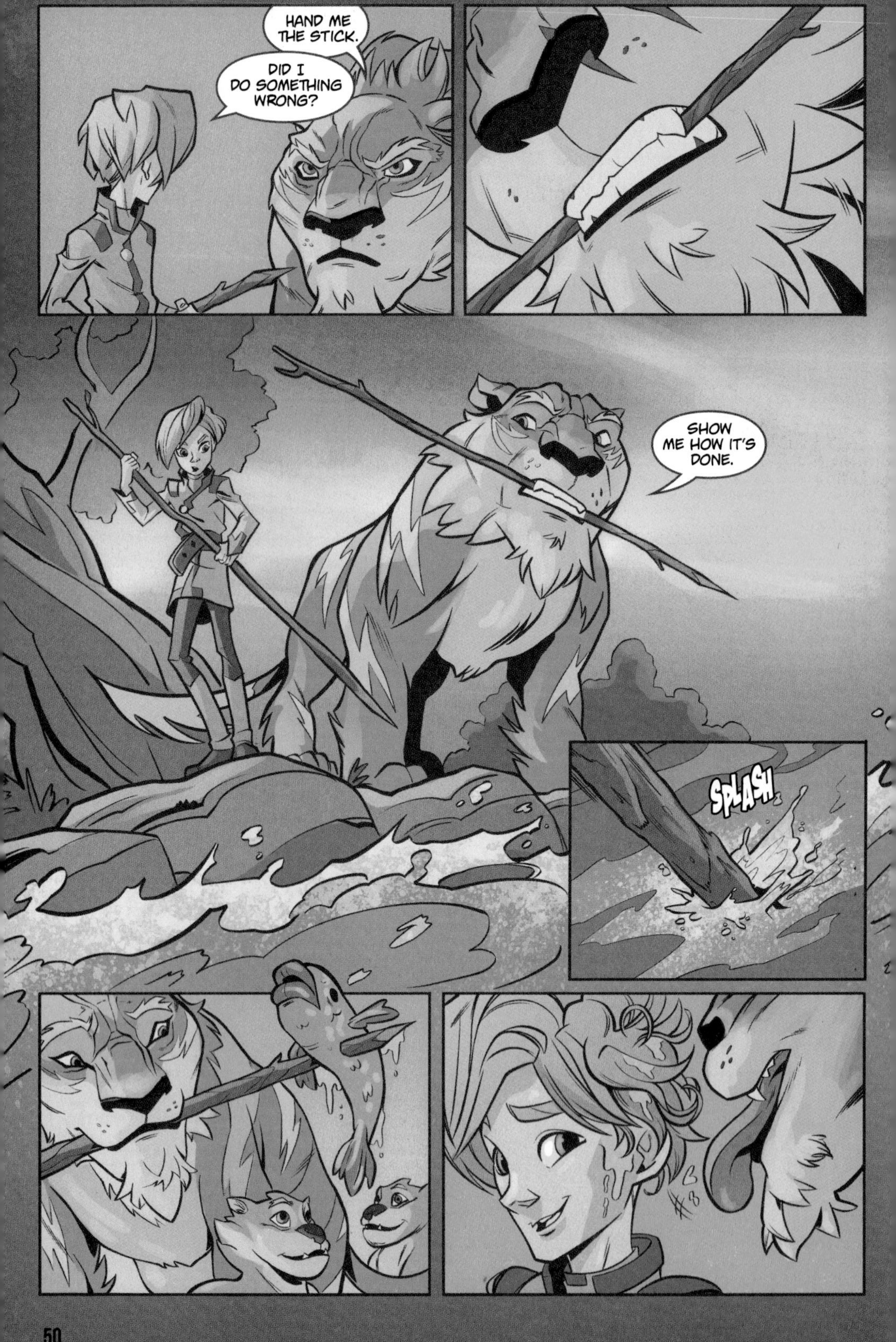
HAND ME THE STICK.
DID I DO SOMETHING WRONG?
SHOW ME HOW IT'S DONE.
SPLASH

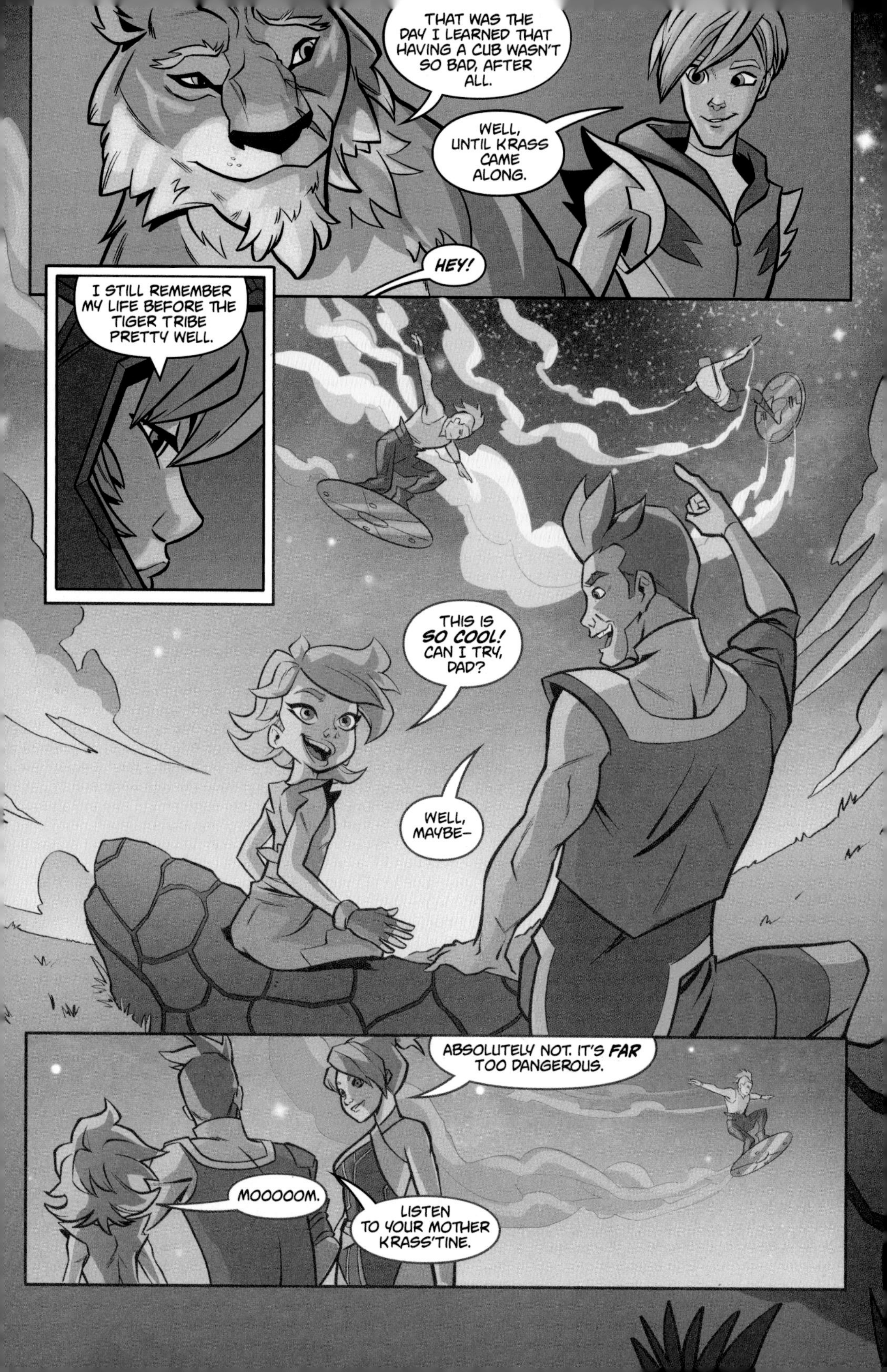
THAT WAS THE DAY I LEARNED THAT HAVING A CUB WASN'T SO BAD, AFTER ALL.
WELL, UNTIL KRASS CAME ALONG.
HEY!
I STILL REMEMBER MY LIFE BEFORE THE TIGER TRIBE PRETTY WELL.
THIS IS *SO COOL!* CAN I TRY, DAD?
WELL, MAYBE–
ABSOLUTELY NOT. IT'S *FAR* TOO DANGEROUS.
MOOOOOM.
LISTEN TO YOUR MOTHER KRASS'TINE.

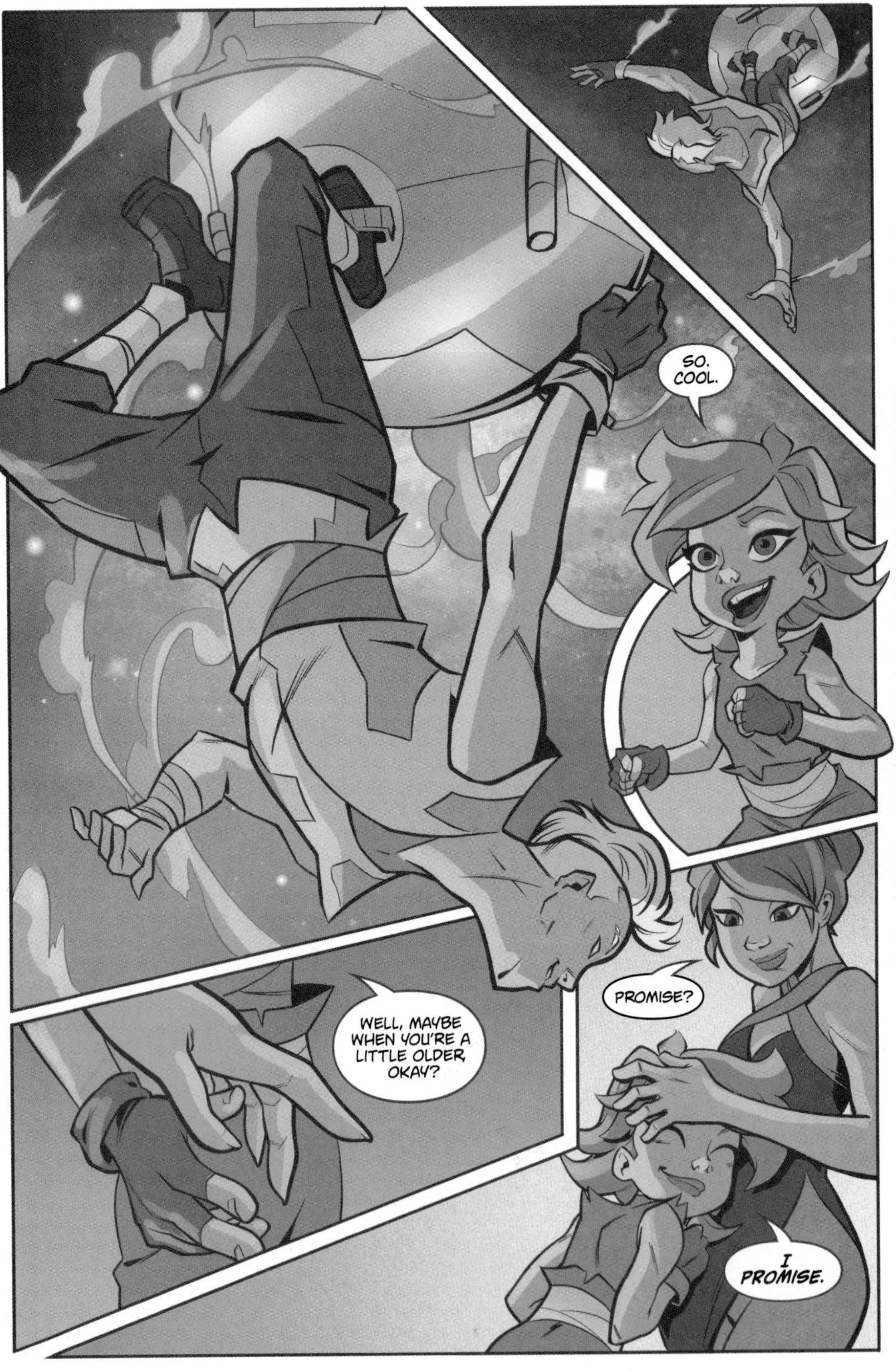
SO. COOL.
WELL, MAYBE WHEN YOU'RE A LITTLE OLDER, OKAY?
PROMISE?
I PROMISE.

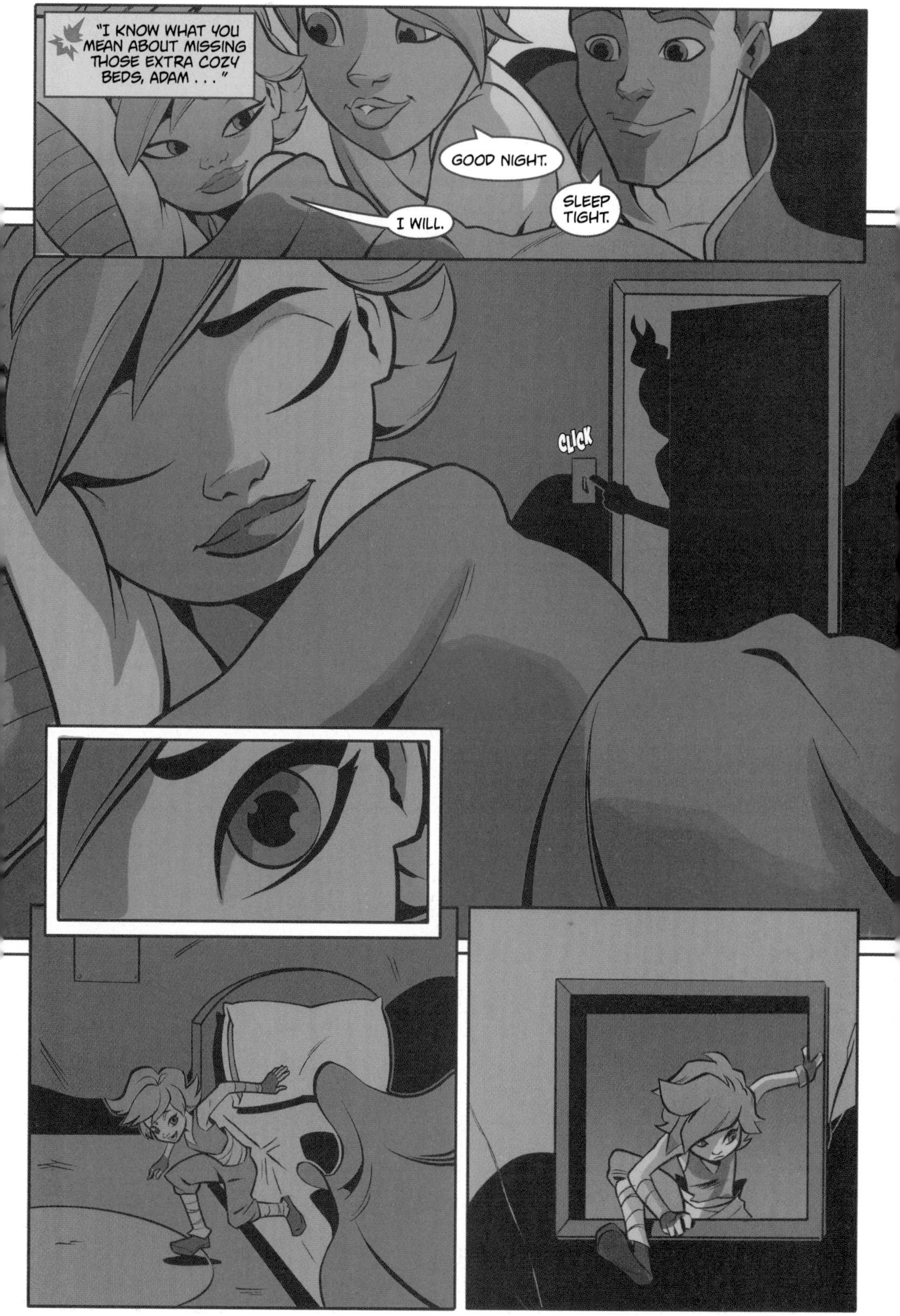
"I KNOW WHAT YOU MEAN ABOUT MISSING THOSE EXTRA COZY BEDS, ADAM . . ."
GOOD NIGHT.
I WILL.
SLEEP TIGHT.
CLICK

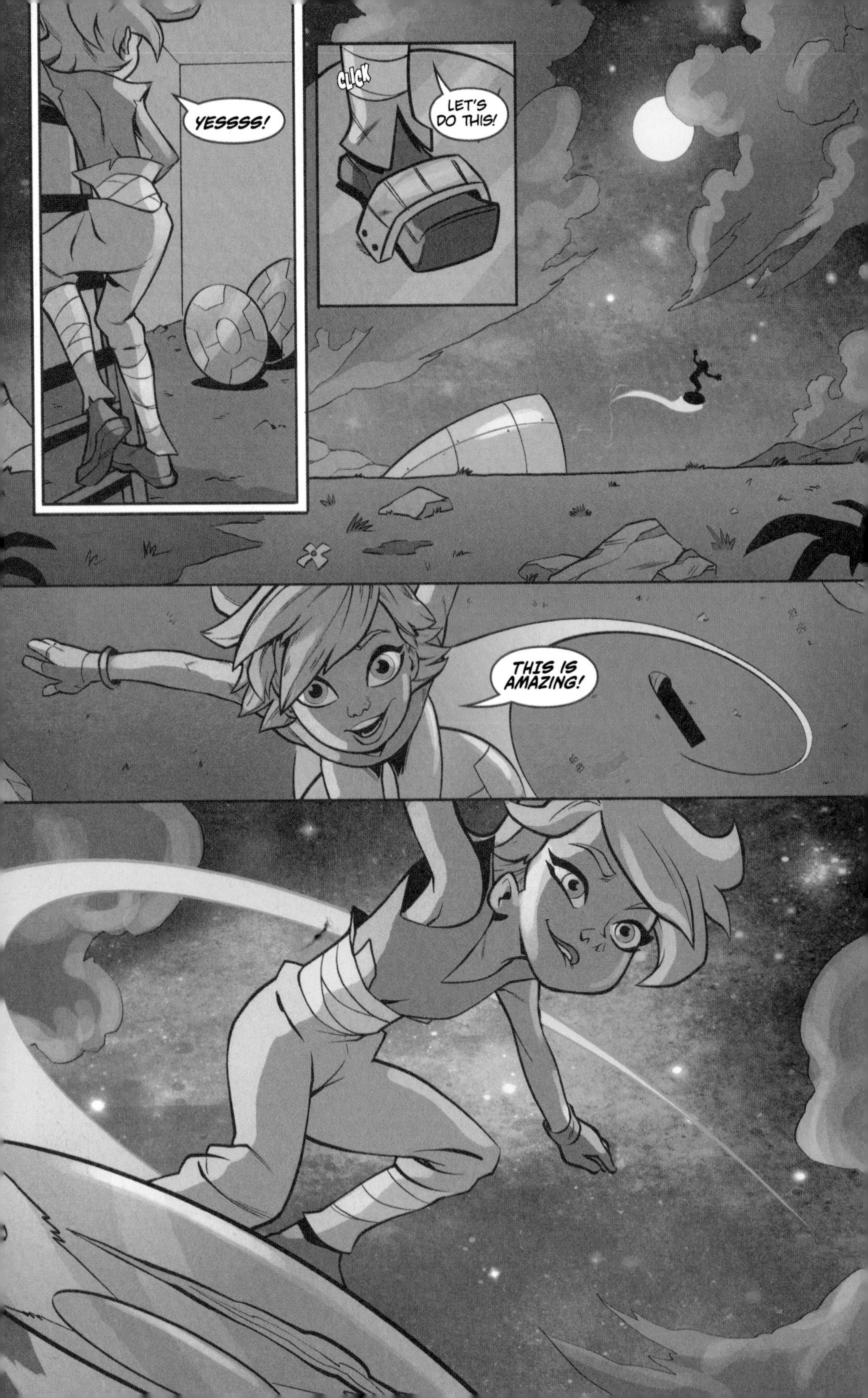
YESSSS!
CLICK
LET'S DO THIS!
THIS IS AMAZING!

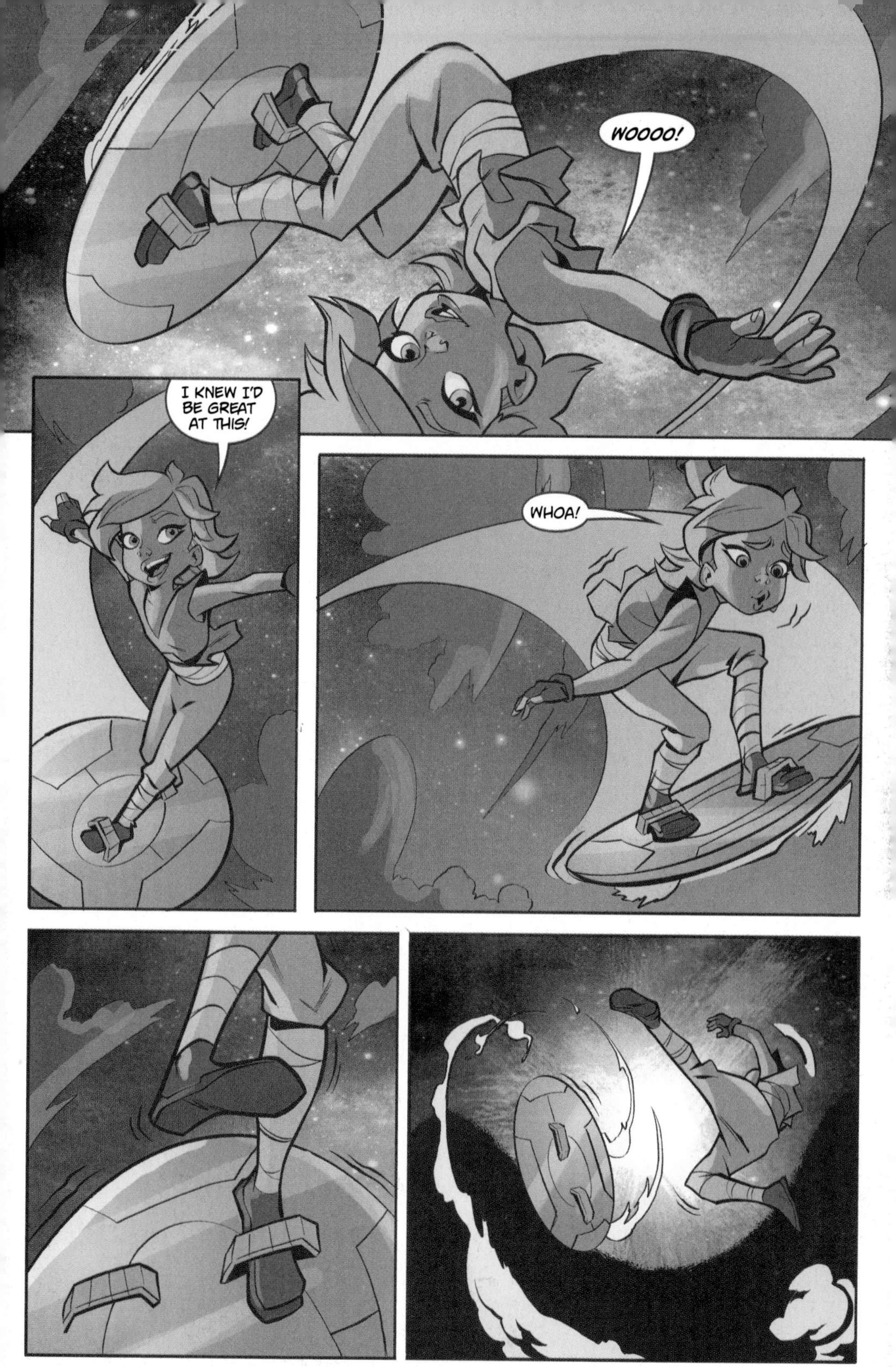
WOOOO!
I KNEW I'D BE GREAT AT THIS!
WHOA!

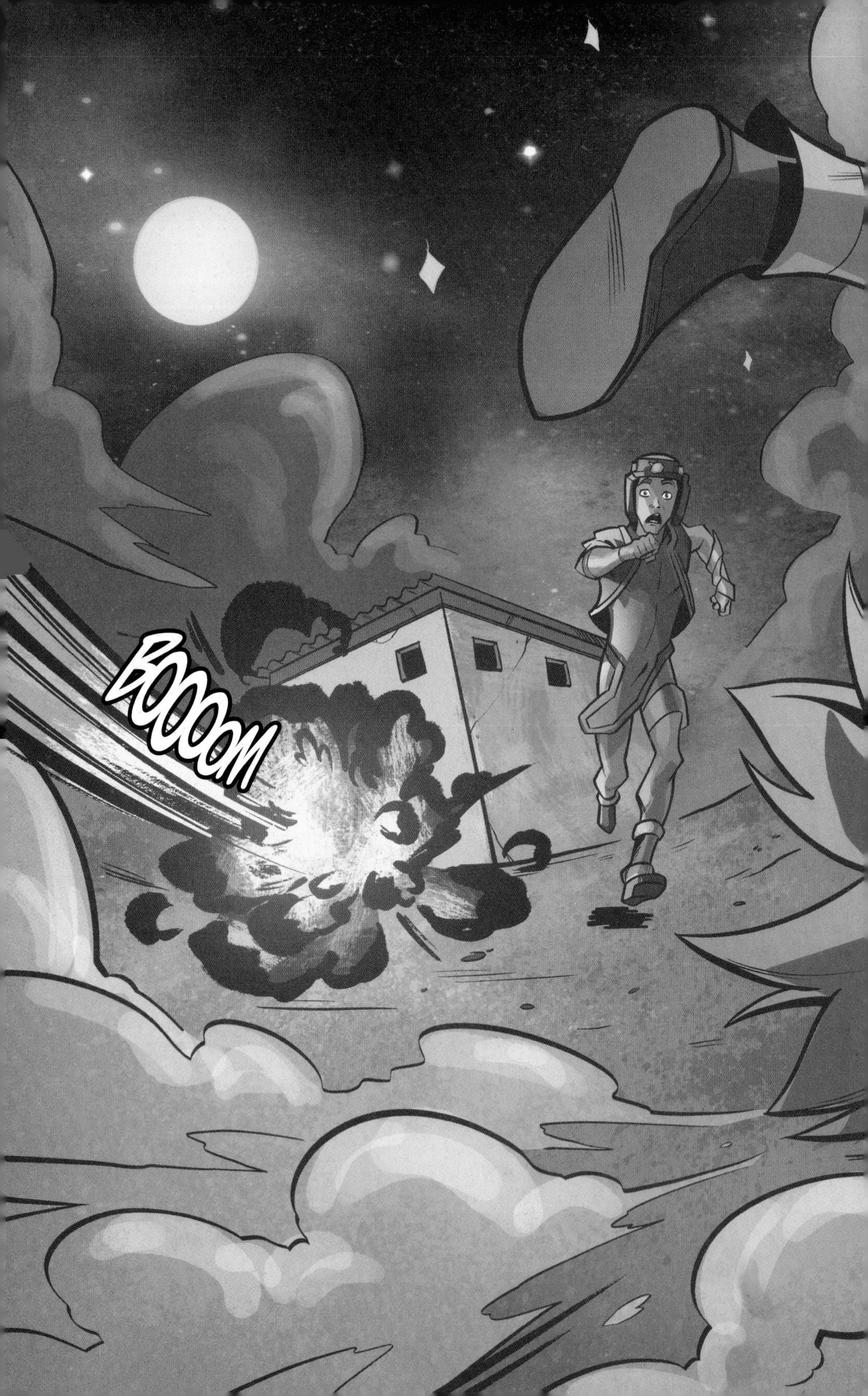
BOOOOM

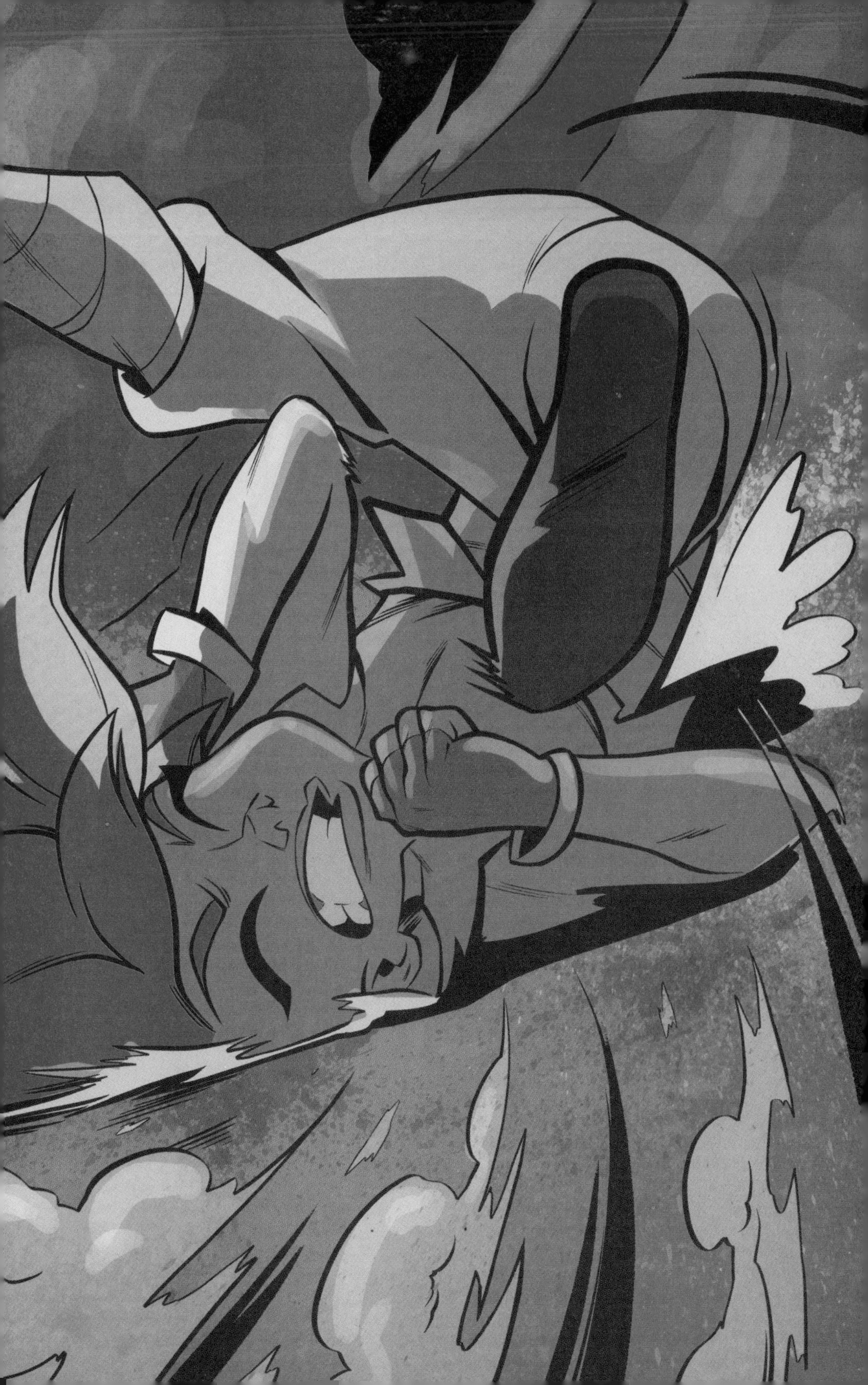

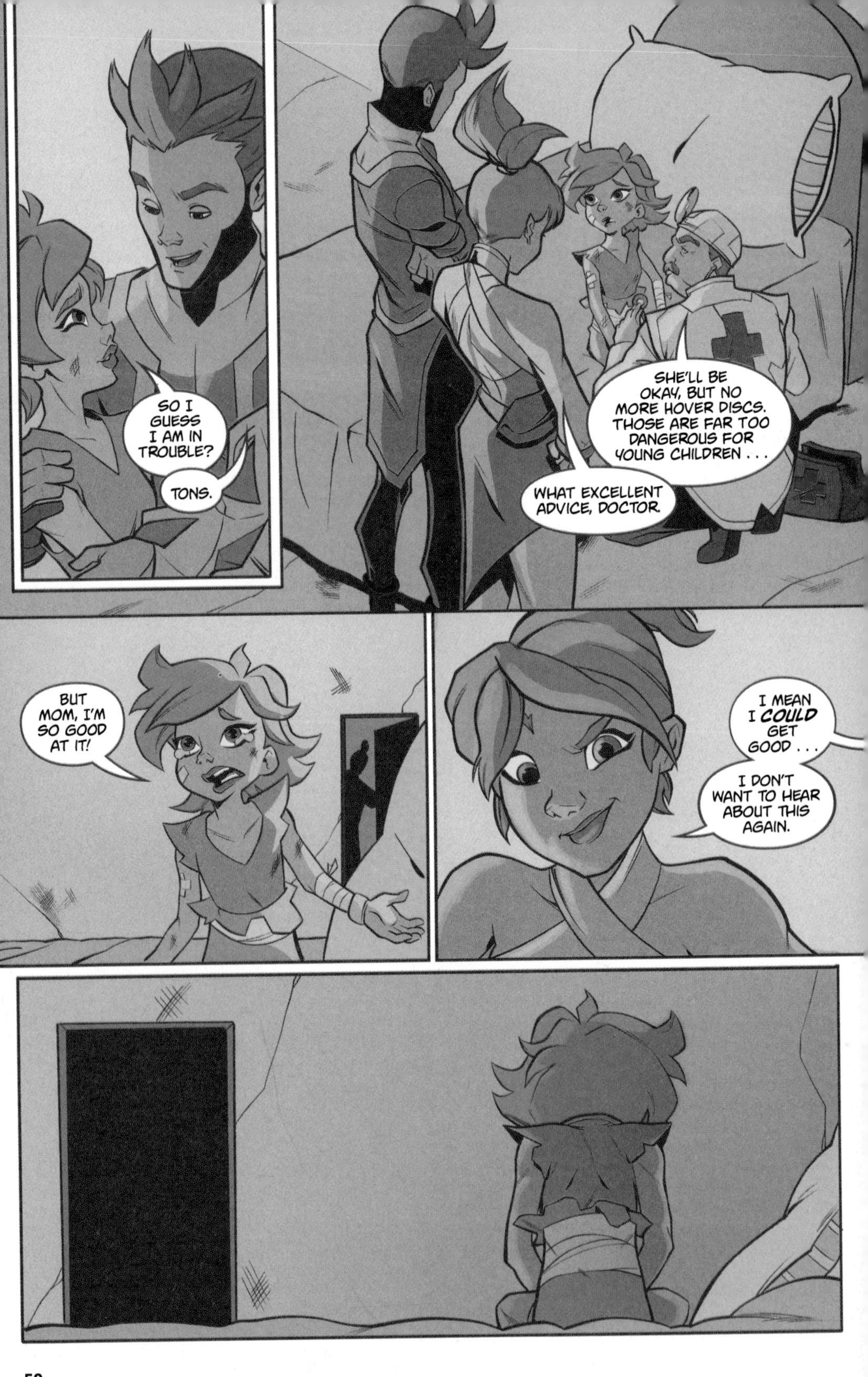
SO I GUESS I AM IN TROUBLE?
TONS.
SHE'LL BE OKAY, BUT NO MORE HOVER DISCS. THOSE ARE FAR TOO DANGEROUS FOR YOUNG CHILDREN . . .
WHAT EXCELLENT ADVICE, DOCTOR.
BUT MOM, I'M SO GOOD AT IT!
I MEAN I **COULD** GET GOOD . . .
I DON'T WANT TO HEAR ABOUT THIS AGAIN.

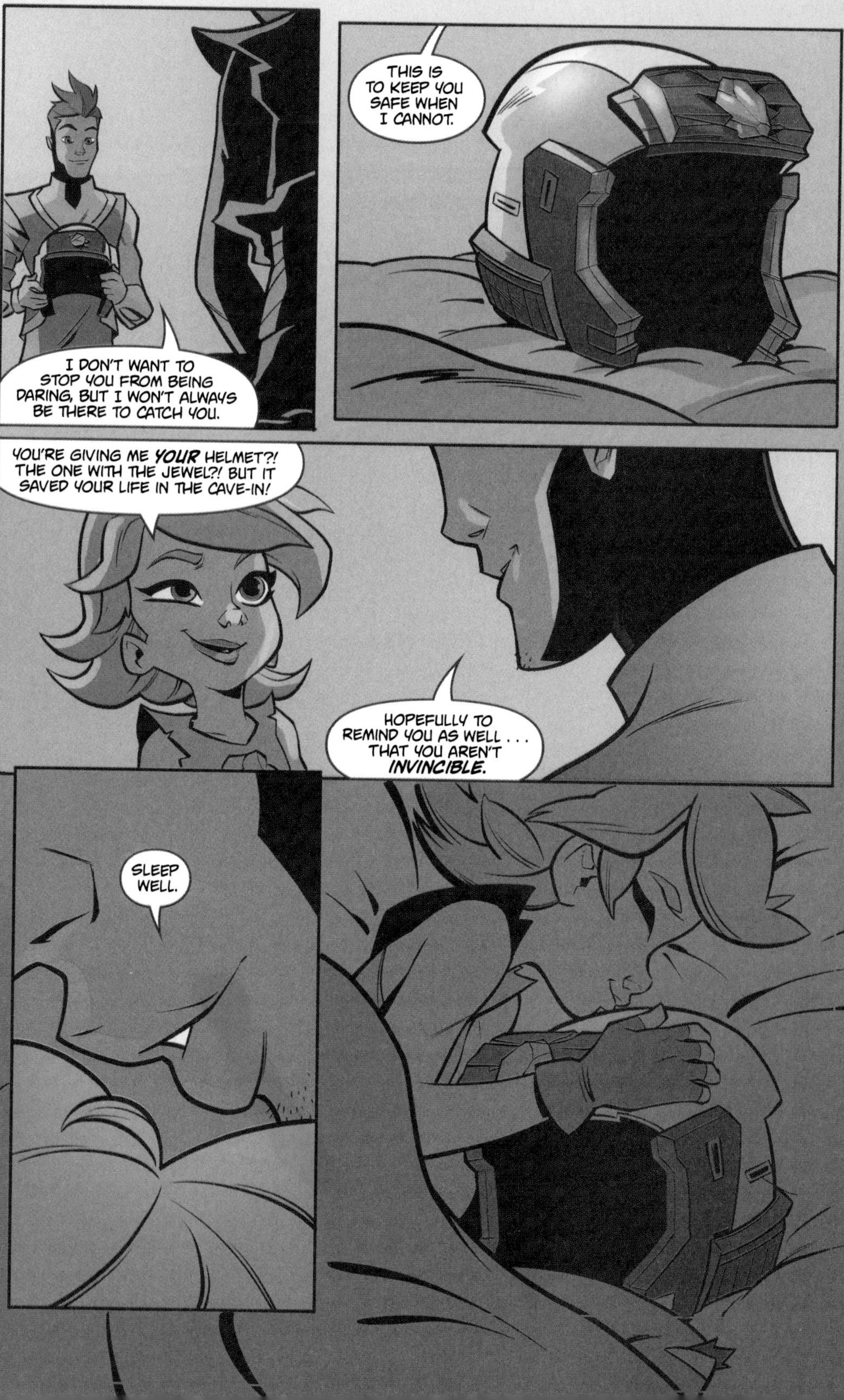
I DON'T WANT TO STOP YOU FROM BEING DARING, BUT I WON'T ALWAYS BE THERE TO CATCH YOU.
THIS IS TO KEEP YOU SAFE WHEN I CANNOT.
YOU'RE GIVING ME YOUR HELMET?! THE ONE WITH THE JEWEL?! BUT IT SAVED YOUR LIFE IN THE CAVE-IN!
HOPEFULLY TO REMIND YOU AS WELL . . . THAT YOU AREN'T INVINCIBLE.
SLEEP WELL.

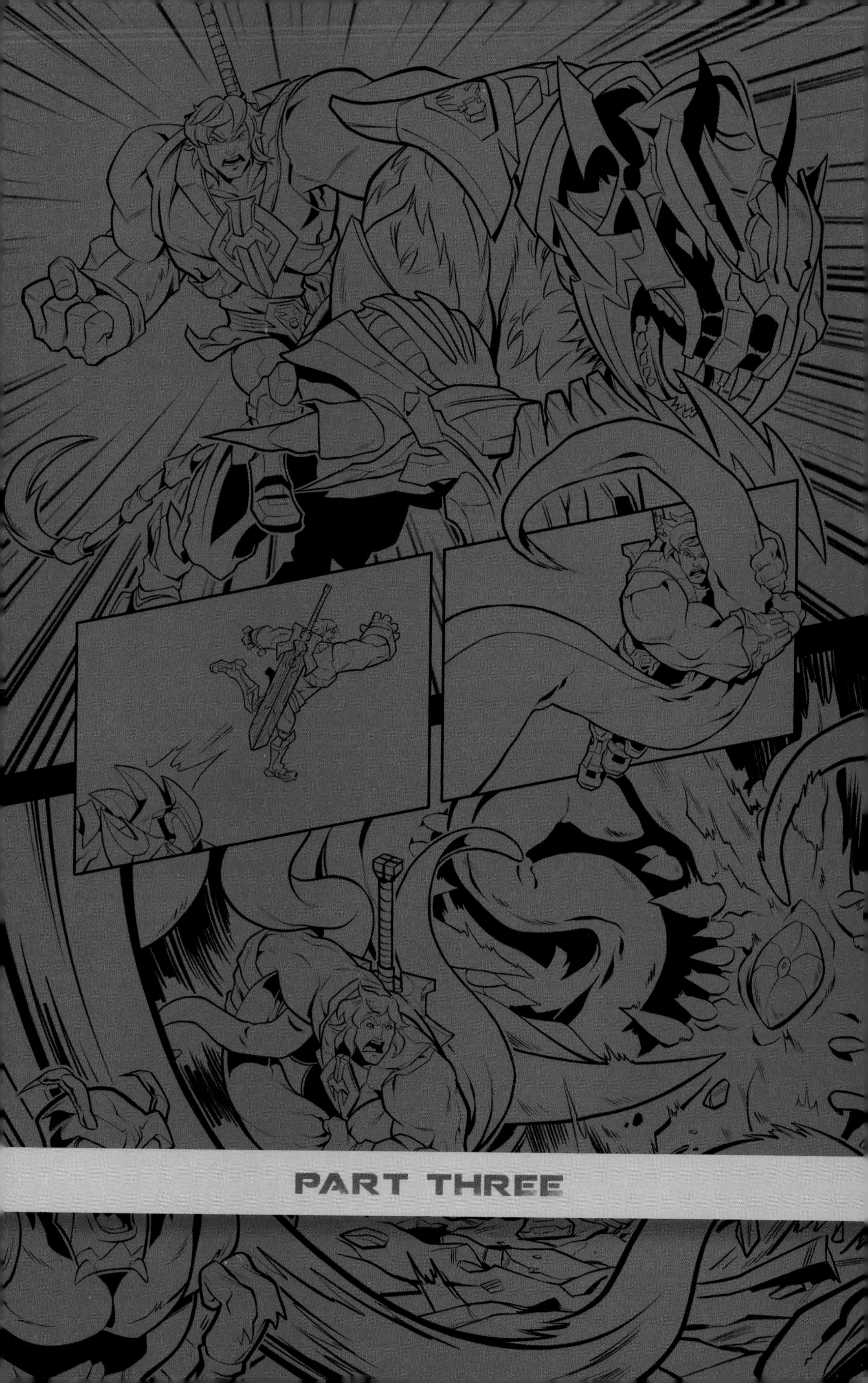

PART THREE

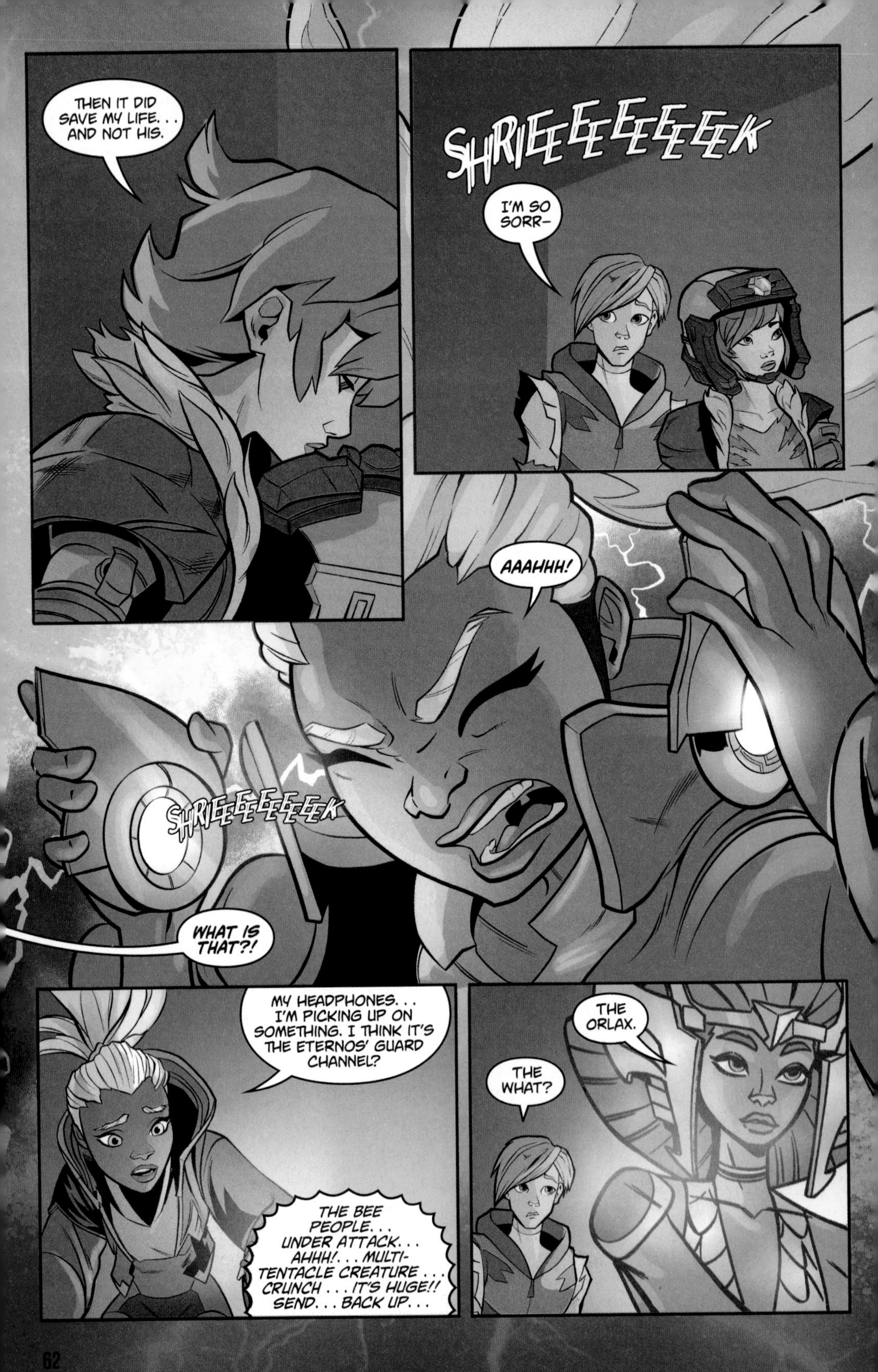
THEN IT DID SAVE MY LIFE. . . AND NOT HIS.
SHRIEEEEEEEEEEK
I'M SO SORR-
AAAHHH!
SHRIEEEEEEEEEK
WHAT IS THAT?!
MY HEADPHONES. . . I'M PICKING UP ON SOMETHING. I THINK IT'S THE ETERNOS' GUARD CHANNEL?
THE BEE PEOPLE. . . UNDER ATTACK. . . AHHH!. . . MULTI-TENTACLE CREATURE . . . CRUNCH . . . IT'S HUGE!! SEND. . . BACK UP. . .
THE ORLAX.
THE WHAT?

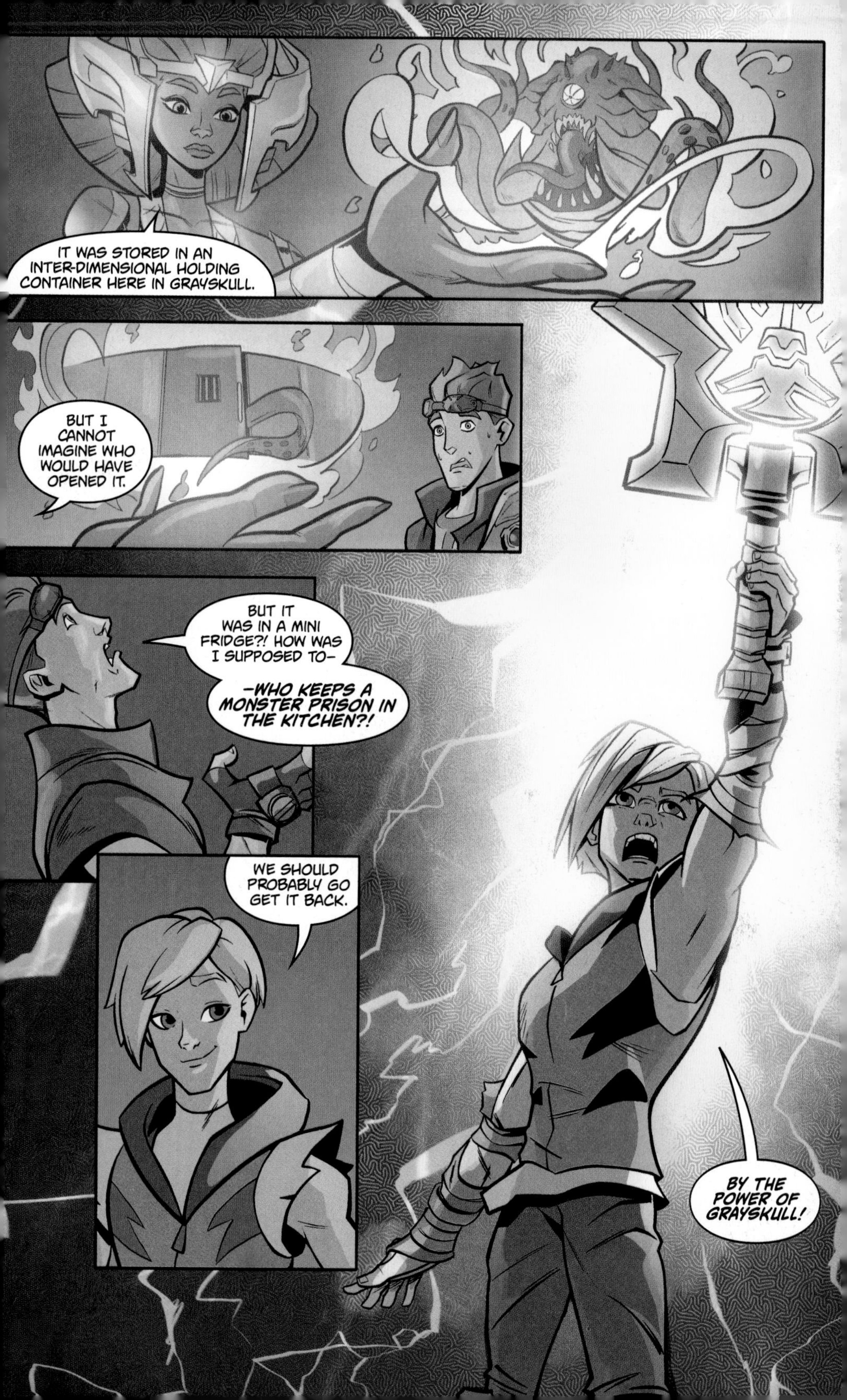
IT WAS STORED IN AN INTER-DIMENSIONAL HOLDING CONTAINER HERE IN GRAYSKULL.
BUT I CANNOT IMAGINE WHO WOULD HAVE OPENED IT.
BUT IT WAS IN A MINI FRIDGE?! HOW WAS I SUPPOSED TO-
-WHO KEEPS A MONSTER PRISON IN THE KITCHEN?!
WE SHOULD PROBABLY GO GET IT BACK.
BY THE POWER OF GRAYSKULL!

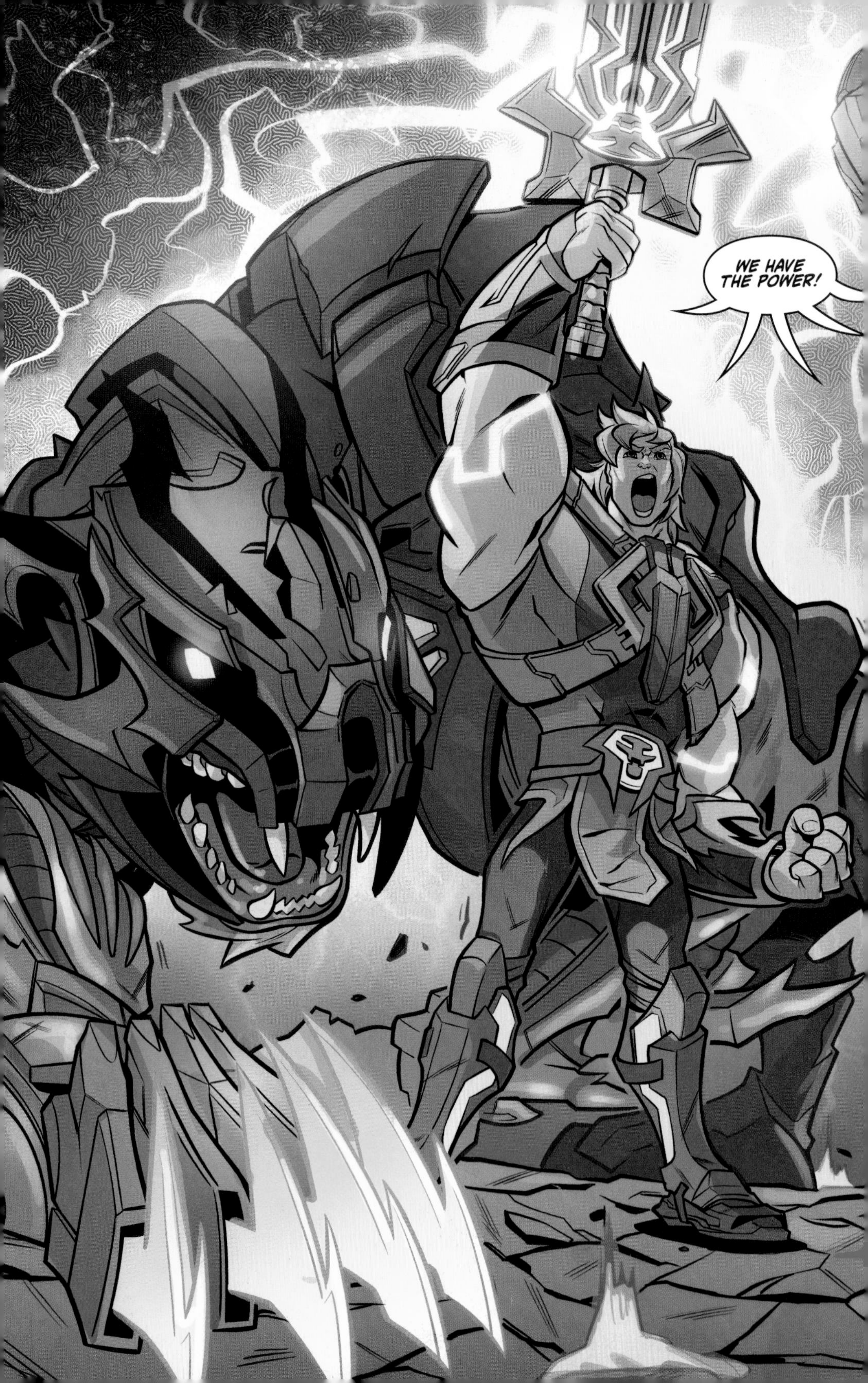
WE HAVE THE POWER!

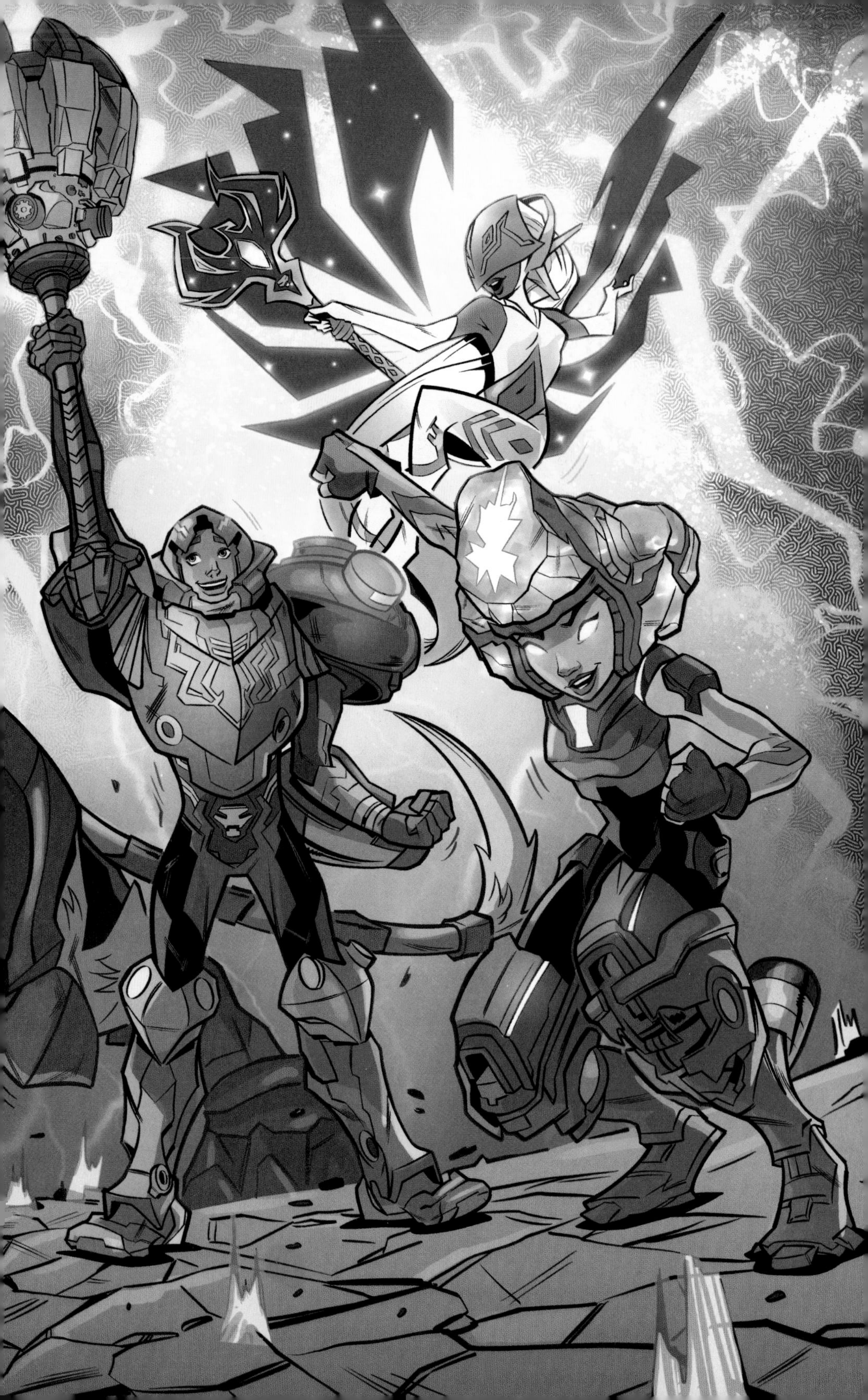

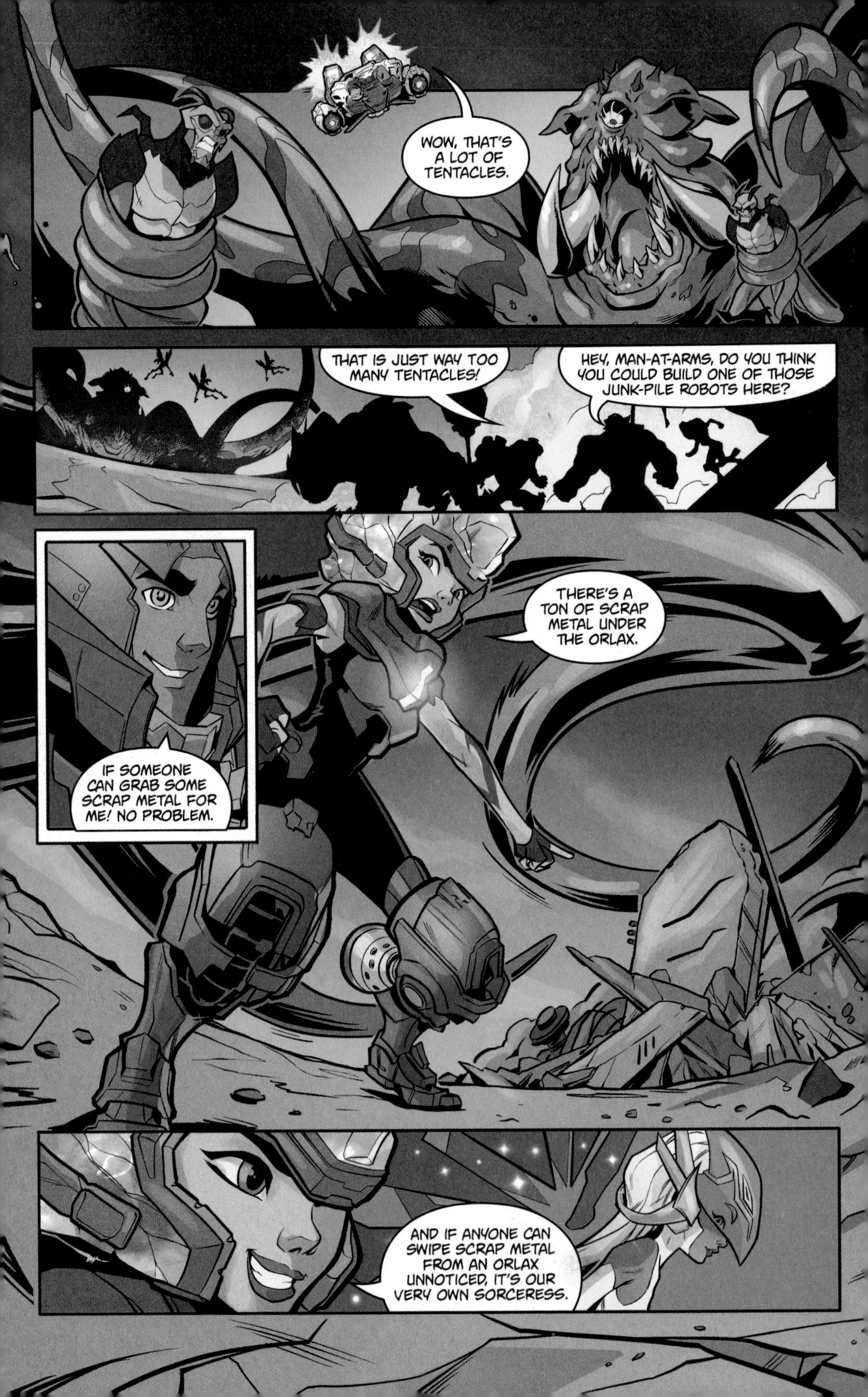
WOW, THAT'S A LOT OF TENTACLES.
THAT IS JUST WAY TOO MANY TENTACLES!
HEY, MAN-AT-ARMS, DO YOU THINK YOU COULD BUILD ONE OF THOSE JUNK-PILE ROBOTS HERE?
IF SOMEONE CAN GRAB SOME SCRAP METAL FOR ME! NO PROBLEM.
THERE'S A TON OF SCRAP METAL UNDER THE ORLAX.
AND IF ANYONE CAN SWIPE SCRAP METAL FROM AN ORLAX UNNOTICED, IT'S OUR VERY OWN SORCERESS.

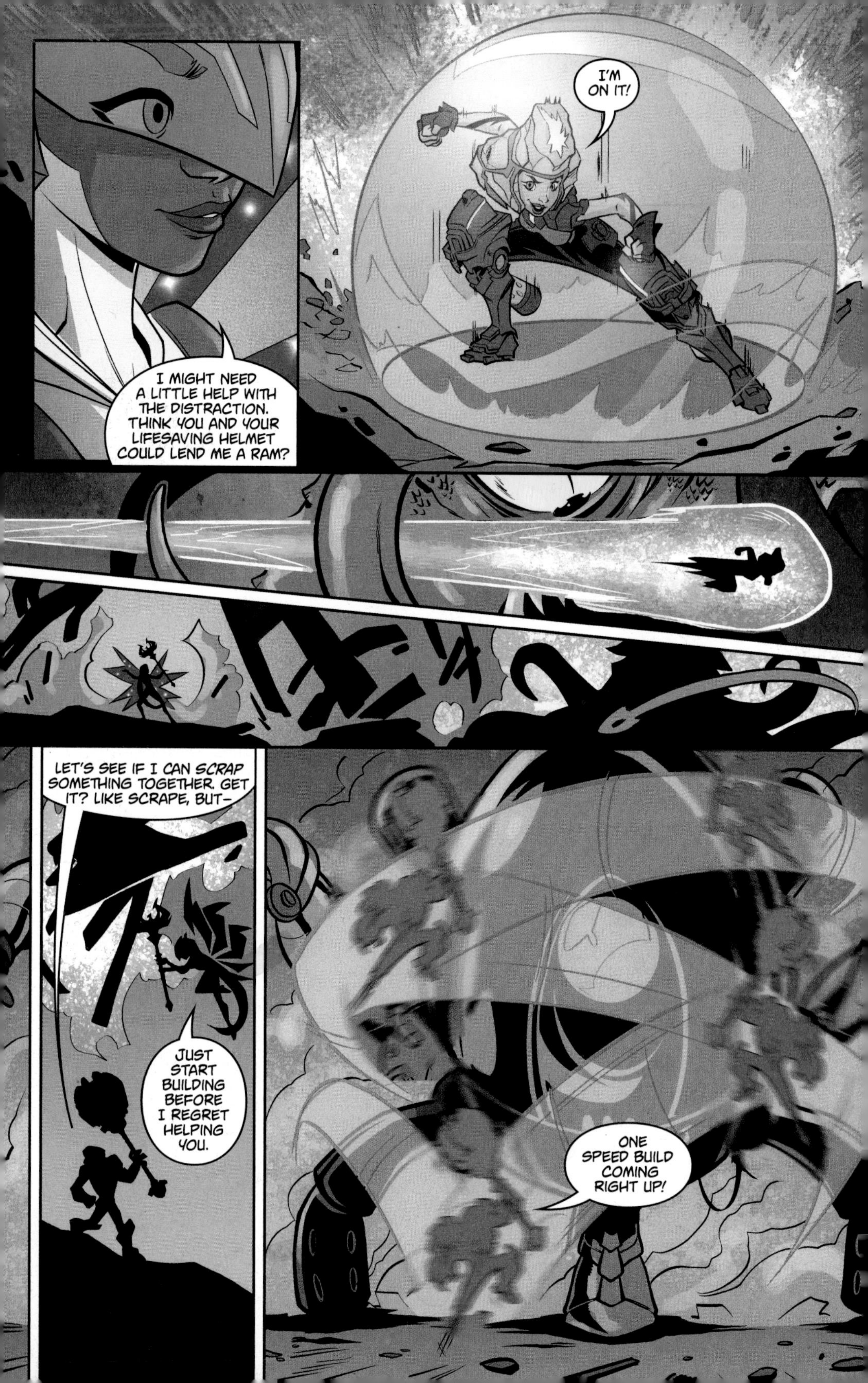
I MIGHT NEED A LITTLE HELP WITH THE DISTRACTION. THINK YOU AND YOUR LIFESAVING HELMET COULD LEND ME A RAM?
I'M ON IT!
LET'S SEE IF I CAN *SCRAP* SOMETHING TOGETHER. GET IT? LIKE SCRAPE, BUT–
JUST START BUILDING BEFORE I REGRET HELPING YOU.
ONE SPEED BUILD COMING RIGHT UP!

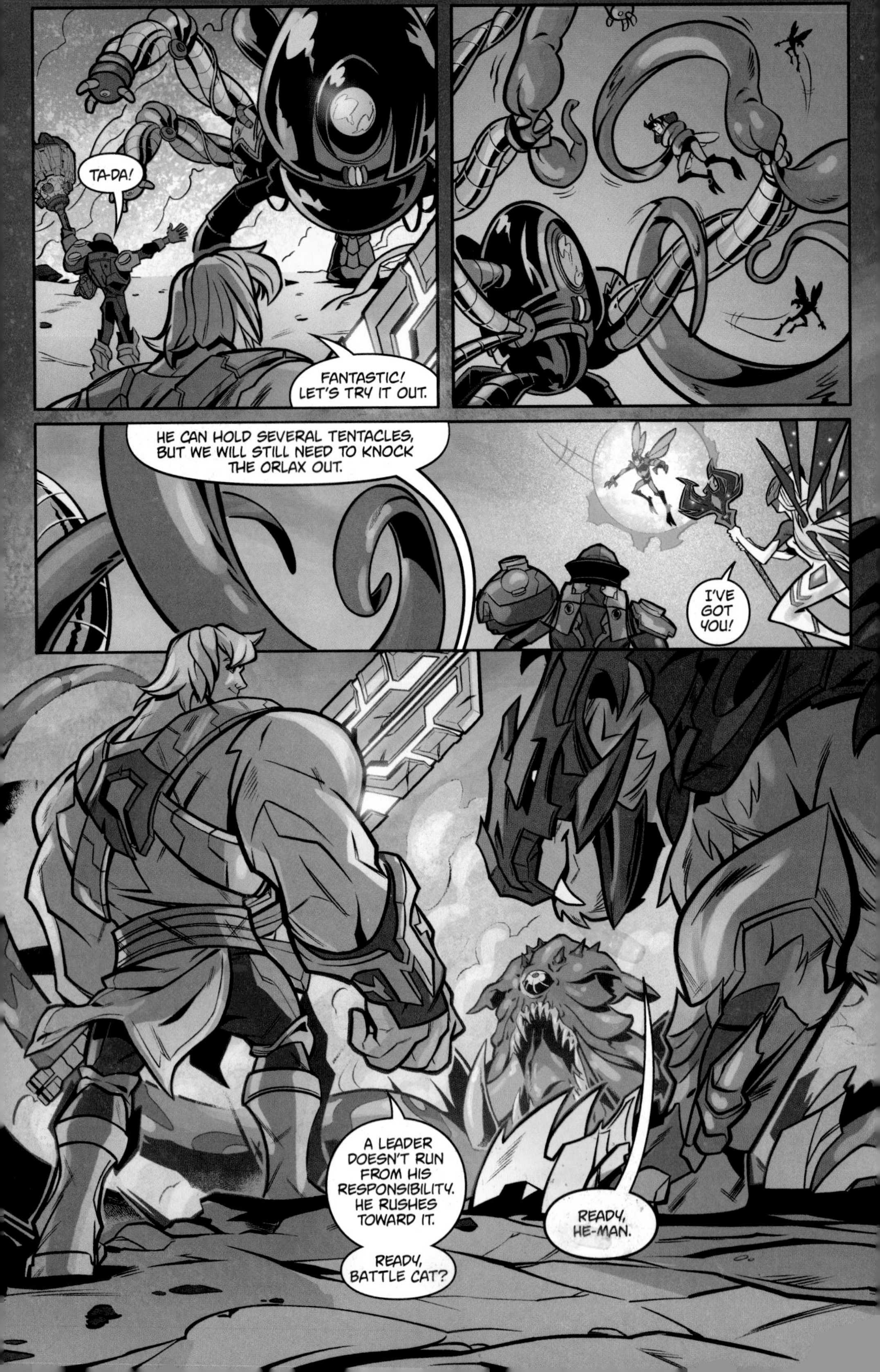
TA-DA!
FANTASTIC! LET'S TRY IT OUT.
HE CAN HOLD SEVERAL TENTACLES, BUT WE WILL STILL NEED TO KNOCK THE ORLAX OUT.
I'VE GOT YOU!
A LEADER DOESN'T RUN FROM HIS RESPONSIBILITY. HE RUSHES TOWARD IT.
READY, BATTLE CAT?
READY, HE-MAN.

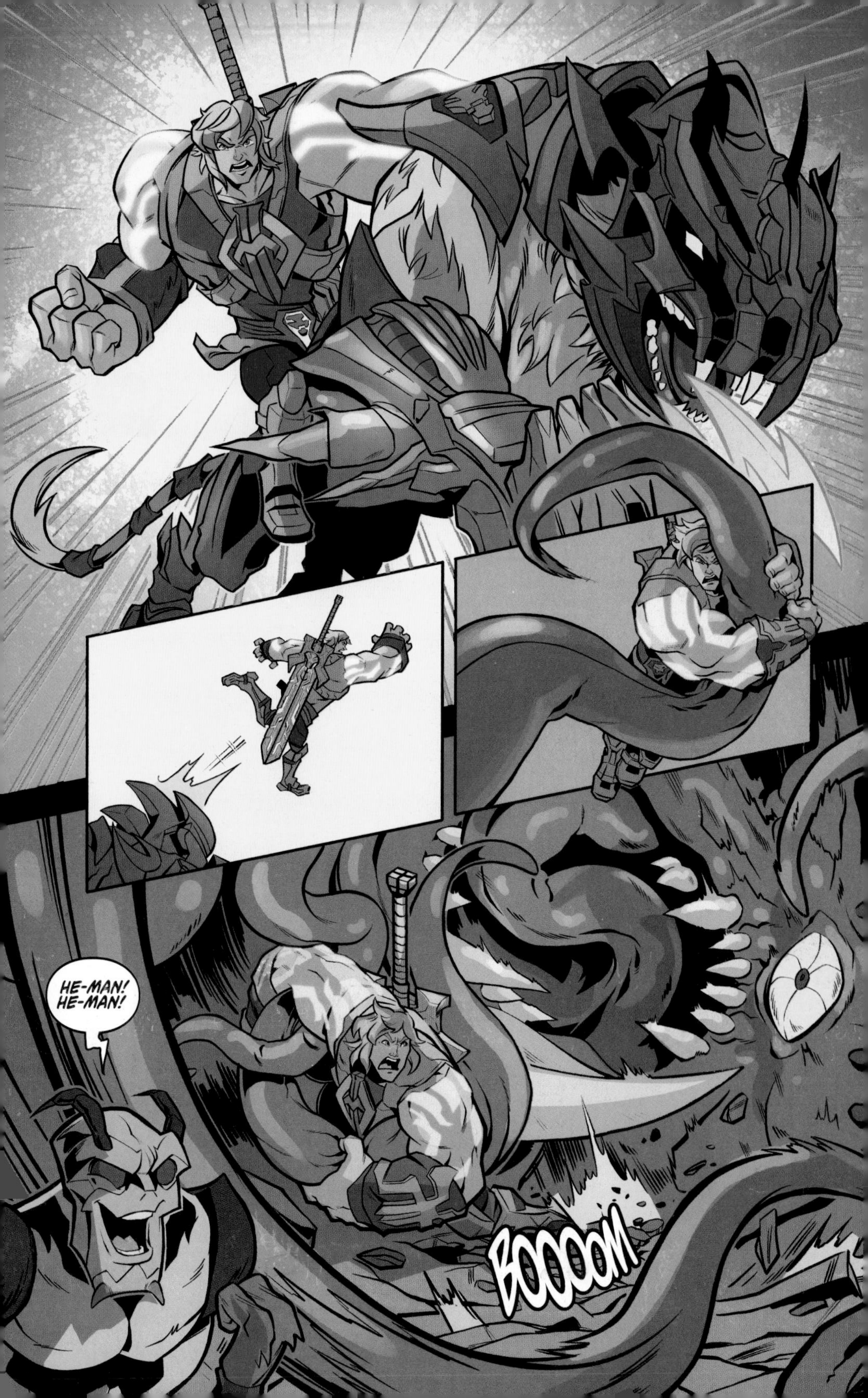
HE-MAN!
HE-MAN!
BOOOOM

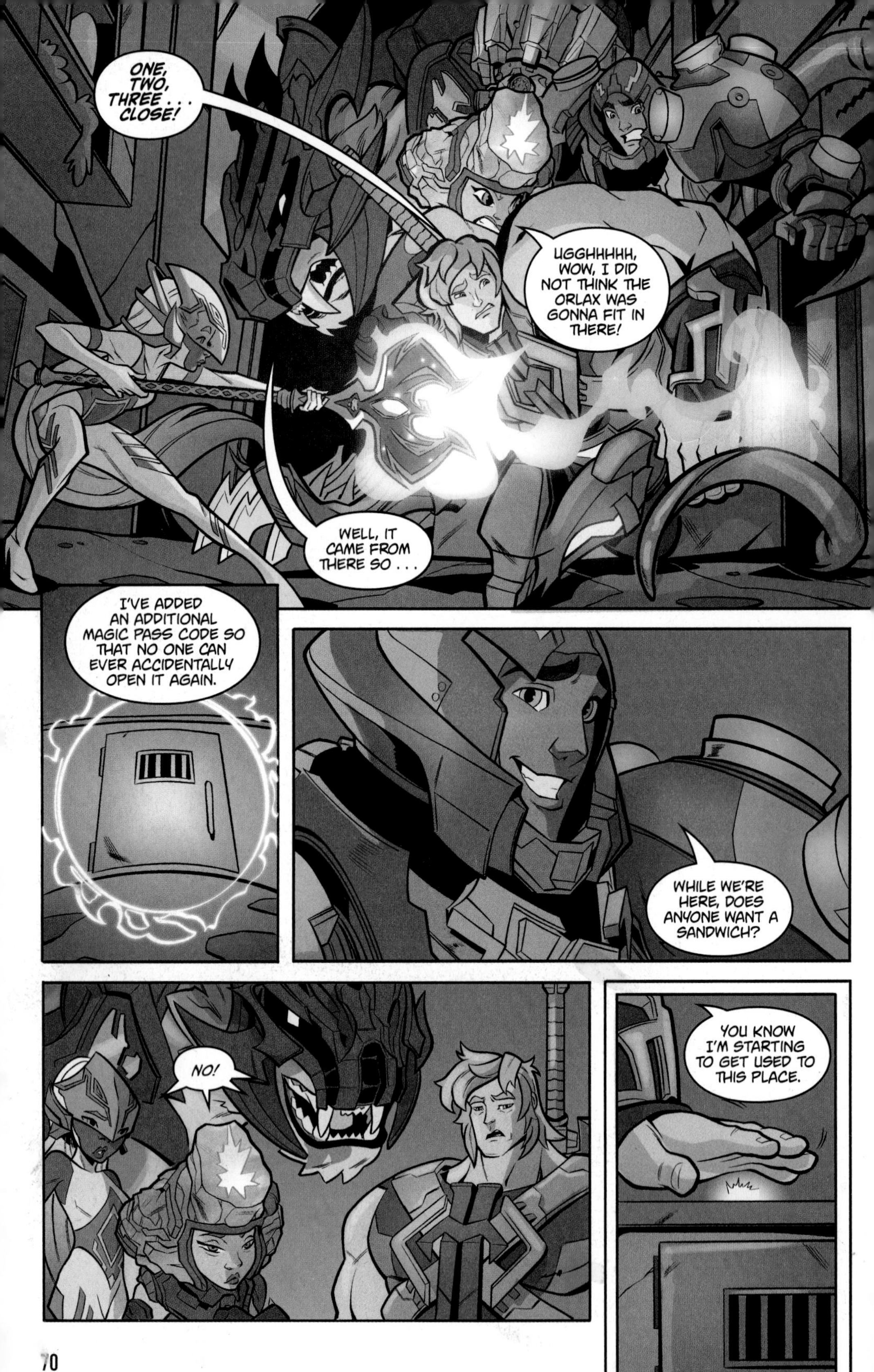
ONE, TWO, THREE . . . CLOSE!
UGGHHHHH, WOW, I DID NOT THINK THE ORLAX WAS GONNA FIT IN THERE!
WELL, IT CAME FROM THERE SO . . .
I'VE ADDED AN ADDITIONAL MAGIC PASS CODE SO THAT NO ONE CAN EVER ACCIDENTALLY OPEN IT AGAIN.
WHILE WE'RE HERE, DOES ANYONE WANT A SANDWICH?
NO!
YOU KNOW I'M STARTING TO GET USED TO THIS PLACE.

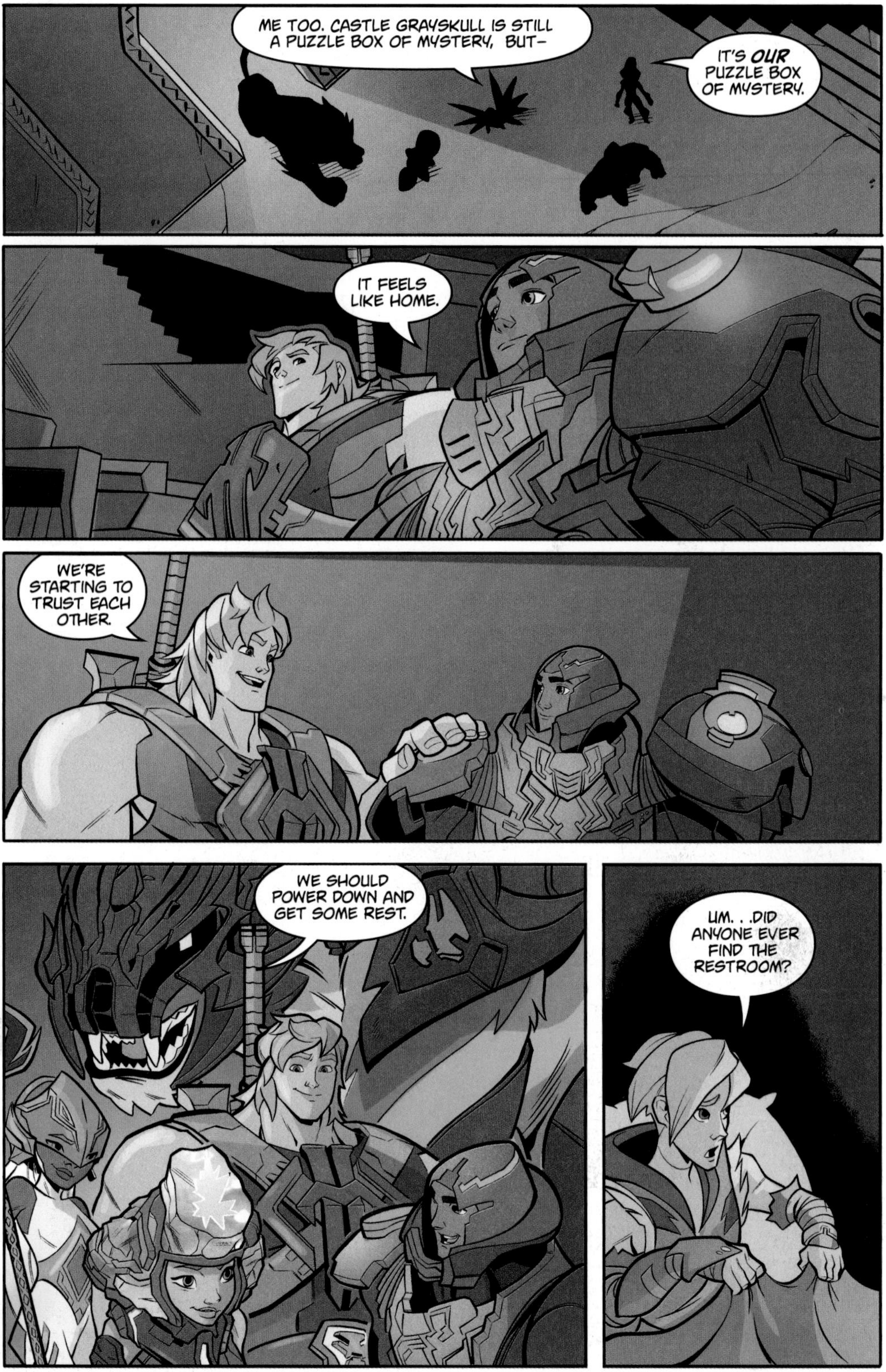

ME TOO. CASTLE GRAYSKULL IS STILL A PUZZLE BOX OF MYSTERY, BUT-
IT'S **OUR** PUZZLE BOX OF MYSTERY.
IT FEELS LIKE HOME.
WE'RE STARTING TO TRUST EACH OTHER.
WE SHOULD POWER DOWN AND GET SOME REST.
UM. . .DID ANYONE EVER FIND THE RESTROOM?

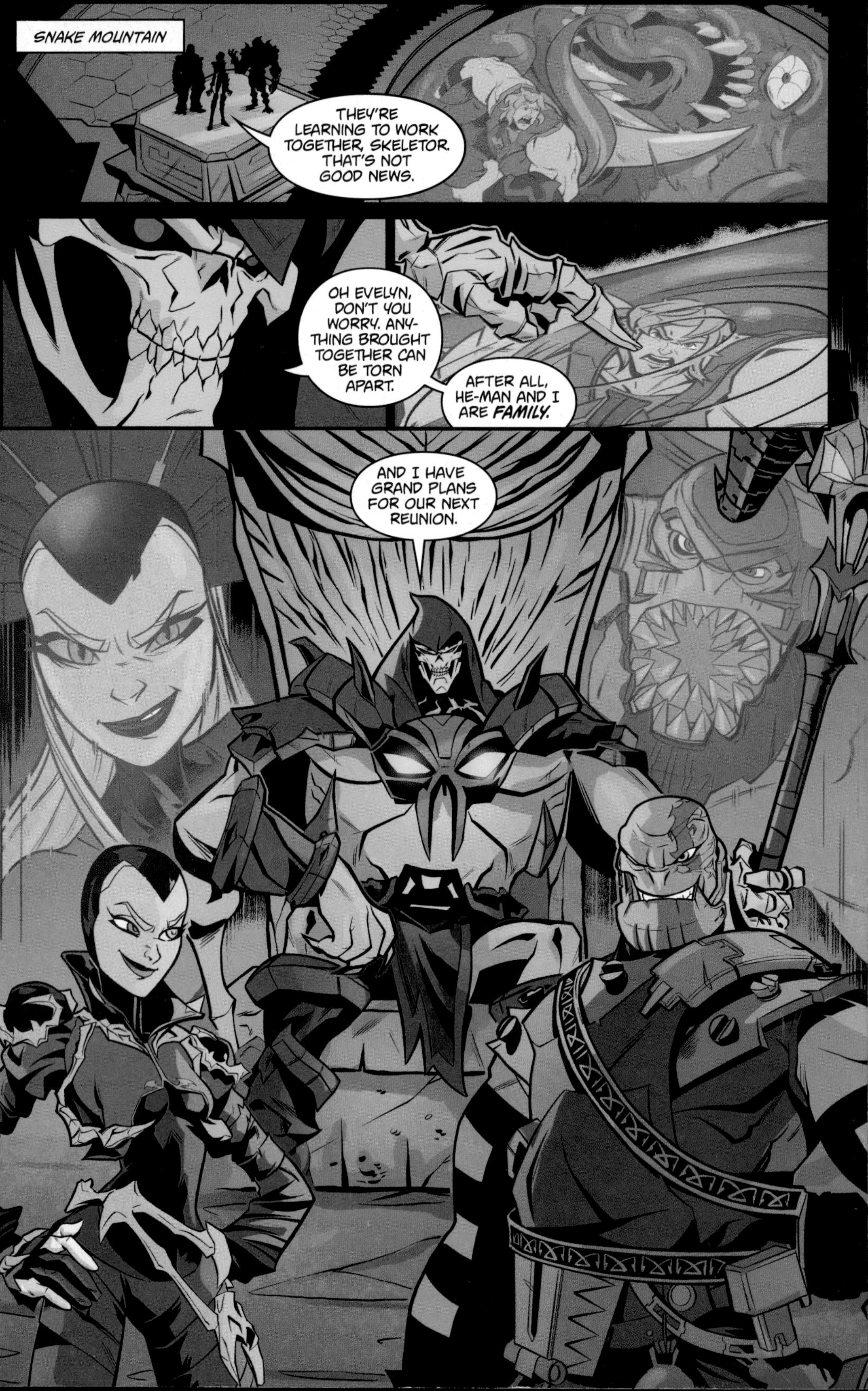
SNAKE MOUNTAIN
THEY'RE LEARNING TO WORK TOGETHER, SKELETOR. THAT'S NOT GOOD NEWS.
OH EVELYN, DON'T YOU WORRY. ANY-THING BROUGHT TOGETHER CAN BE TORN APART.
AFTER ALL, HE-MAN AND I ARE *FAMILY.*
AND I HAVE GRAND PLANS FOR OUR NEXT REUNION.

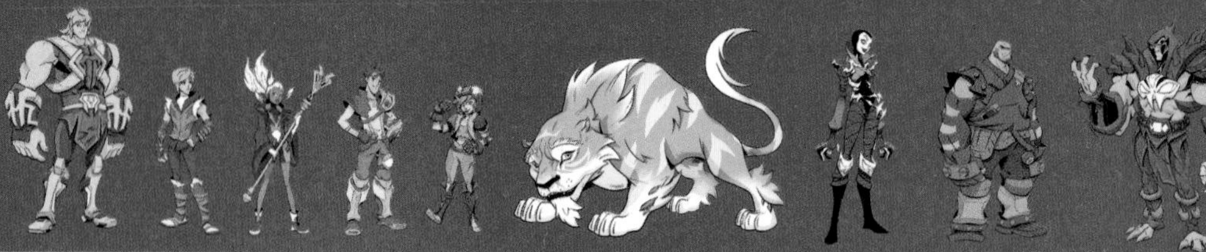

CREATOR BIO PAGE

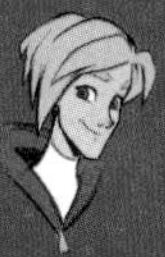

AMANDA DEIBERT - WRITER

AMANDA DEIBERT IS A *NEW YORK TIMES*-BESTSELLING COMIC BOOK AND TELEVISION WRITER. HER COMIC BOOK WRITING INCLUDES MANY TITLES FOR DC COMICS INCLUDING *DC SUPER HERO GIRLS, FLASH FACTS, WONDER WOMAN: AGENT OF PEACE, TEEN TITANS GO!, WONDER WOMAN '77,* AND *BATMAN AND HARLEY QUINN* AS WELL AS WORK FOR STORM KING COMICS, DYNAMITE COMICS, MCCLELLAND & STEWART, AND OTHERS. SHE IS CURRENTLY WRITING *HE-MAN AND THE MASTERS OF THE UNIVERSE* FOR NETFLIX. OTHER TV CREDITS INCLUDE WORK FOR CBS, SYFY, OWN, PIVOT, HULU, AND FOUR YEARS FOR FORMER VICE PRESIDENT AL GORE'S 24 HOURS OF REALITY.

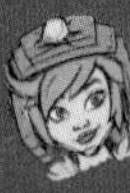

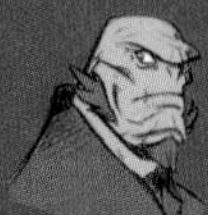

MIKE ANDERSON - ARTIST

MIKE IS A FREELANCE COMIC BOOK ARTIST AND ILLUSTRATOR FROM EDMOND, OKLAHOMA. MIKE IS A PROUD HUSBAND TO HIS WIFE, HEATHER, AND FATHER TO HIS 3 BOYS COLT, KODA, AND CADEN. MIKE HAS DONE WORK FOR SEVERAL INDIE AND MAIN-STREAM COMIC PUBLISHERS, AS WELL AS ILLUSTRATION AND ANIMATION WORK FOR MANY NATIONAL BRANDS. BORN IN 1985, MIKE IS A FAN OF ALL THINGS 80S AND 90S, AND THE COMICS AND CARTOONS OF THOSE DECADES ARE WHAT SPAWNED HIS LOVE OF DRAWING AND ANIMATION. NEEDLESS TO SAY, GETTING TO DRAW A HE-MAN GRAPHIC NOVEL HAS BECOME A DREAM COME TRUE. WHEN MIKE ISN'T DRAWING COMICS, HE ENJOYS ROUGHHOUSING WITH HIS SONS, COLLECTING TOYS AND COMICS, ANIMATING, COLLECTING TOYS, CELEBRATING HALLOWEEN ALL YEAR-LONG, COLLECTING TOYS, PODCASTING, AND EVEN COLLECTING TOYS. YOU CAN FIND MORE OF MIKE'S COMIC WORK ON MIKEYCOMIX.COM

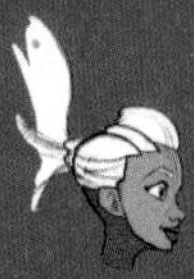

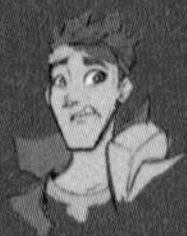

ROB DAVID - STORY

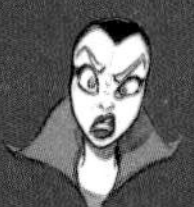

ROB DAVID IS THE EXECUTIVE PRODUCER AND SHOWRUNNER OF THE NETFLIX HIT SERIES *HE-MAN AND THE MASTERS OF THE UNIVERSE*, WHICH HE ALSO DEVELOPED FOR TELEVISION. AS A DYNAMIC STORYTELLER, HE HAS WORKED ACROSS FILM, TELEVISION, PUBLISHING, AND MOBILE GAMES, WRITING AND PRODUCING KIDS AND FAMILY CONTENT FOR NETFLIX, DISNEY, CARTOON NETWORK, NICKELODEON, PBS, AND MORE. A GRADUATE OF COLUMBIA UNIVERSITY WITH A B.A. IN PHILOSOPHY, HE VALUES STORIES THAT CAPTURE LIFE IN ITS FULLEST: VISCERAL, EMOTIONAL, AND GUT-BUSTING FUN. HIS WRITING HAS RUN THE GAMUT, FROM COMEDY, ACTION-ADVENTURE SERIES—SUCH AS THE TEENAGE MUTANT NINJA TURTLES 25TH ANNIVERSARY FEATURE-LENGTH SPECIAL *TURTLES FOREVER*, TO PRESCHOOL HITS—SUCH AS NICK JR.'S *WOW! WOW! WUBBZY!*, TO COMIC BOOKS—SUCH AS THE CRITICALLY ACCLAIMED *HE-MAN: THE ETERNITY WAR* PUBLISHED BY DC COMICS. IN HIS ROLE AS VICE PRESIDENT AT MATTEL TELEVISION, ROB OVERSEES CREATIVE FOR ALL MATTEL INTELLECTUAL PROPERTIES. PRIOR TO *HE-MAN AND THE MASTERS OF THE UNIVERSE*, HE CO-DEVELOPED AND EXECUTIVE PRODUCED THE NETFLIX SERIES *MASTERS OF THE UNIVERSE: REVELATION*.

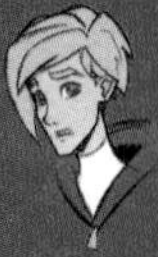

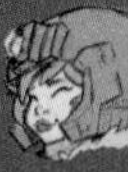

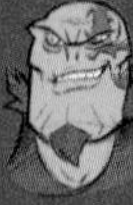

BRAD SIMPRON - COLORIST

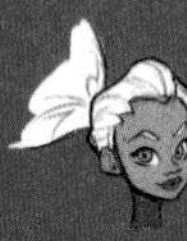

BRAD SIMPSON'S DISTINCT COLOR ART HAS APPEARED IN NUMEROUS TITLES INCLUDING *THE AMAZING SPIDERMAN, 30 DAYS OF NIGHT*, AND IN THE CURRENT MONTHLY SERIES *COFFIN BOUND*. HE RESIDES IN ASHLAND, OREGON, WITH HIS WIFE, SARAH, AND SONS, CLIVE AND MADDOX. WHEN HE IS NOT ON A DEADLINE, HE ENJOYS ANTICIPATING FUTURE DEADLINES.

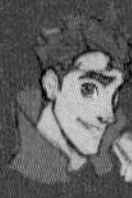

DEZI SIENTY - LETTERER

DEZI SIENTY HAS BEEN WORKING IN COMICS FOR FIFTEEN YEARS. HE'S MOSTLY KNOWN AS A LETTERER AND A PRODUCTION EDITOR. HIS PAST CLIENTS INCLUDE DC ENTERTAINMENT, KODANSHA, ASPEN, FIRST SECOND, IDW, RANDOM HOUSE, AND SCHOLASTIC. HE IS A LIFELONG HE-MAN FAN AND IS VERY THANKFUL TO SCHOLASTIC FOR MAKING HIS NINE-YEAR-OLD DREAMS COME TRUE. YOU CAN FIND DEZI'S WORK AT WWW.DEZICNT.COM.

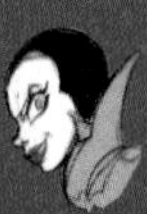